W9-BRT-552

Gerber ran toward the far end of the redoubt

He passed the dispensary and the team house, which were little more than smoking rubble now. He found Fulton crouched there, a PRC-25 set up on top of the bunker, giving the antenna a little extra height.

"How are we doing?" asked Gerber.

"Not good. I've ordered the strikers on the west wall to N and E. Can't get them in here, and their only hope is to escape. We've lost the whole outer perimeter."

"What's our status now?"

Fulton laughed. "Well, the Mike Force is still on the ground at Moc Hoa. Seems the rain has the choppers grounded. The Air Force can't penetrate the clouds, and most of the artillery around here is involved in counterbattery duels. Charlie is dropping mortars on everything within range of us."

"Then we're on our own," said Gerber grimly.

"That's about the size of it."

"... Vietnam: Ground Zero . . . are books to linger in the mind long after their reading."

—*Midwest Book Review*

Also available by Eric Helm:

VIETNAM: GROUND ZERO
P.O.W.
UNCONFIRMED KILL
THE FALL OF CAMP A-555
SOLDIER'S MEDAL
THE KIT CARSON SCOUT
THE HOBO WOODS
GUIDELINES
THE VILLE

VIETNAM: GROUND ZERO™

INCIDENT AT PLEI SOI

ERIC HELM

Lincoln Middle School
School District 64
164 S. Prospect Ave.
Park Ridge, IL 60068

A GOLD EAGLE BOOK FROM

W❂RLDWIDE®

TORONTO • NEW YORK • LONDON • PARIS
AMSTERDAM • STOCKHOLM • HAMBURG
ATHENS • MILAN • TOKYO • SYDNEY

First edition February 1988

ISBN 0-373-62710-6

Copyright © 1988 by Eric Helm.
Philippine copyright 1988. Australian copyright 1988.

All rights reserved. Except for use in any review, the
reproduction or utilization of this work in whole or in part
in any form by any electronic, mechanical or other means,
now known or hereafter invented, including xerography,
photocopying and recording, or in any information storage
or retrieval system, is forbidden without the permission
of the publisher, Worldwide Library, 225 Duncan Mill Road,
Don Mills, Ontario, Canada M3B 3K9.

All the characters in this book have no existence outside the
imagination of the author and have no relation whatsoever to
anyone bearing the same name or names. They are not even
distantly inspired by any individual known or unknown to the
author, and all the incidents are pure invention.

® are Trademarks registered in the United States Patent and
Trademark Office and in other countries. T.M. are Trademarks;
registration applied for in the United States Patent and Trademark
Office and in other countries.

Printed in Canada

VIETNAM: GROUND ZERO.™

INCIDENT AT PLEI SOI

PROLOGUE

Tan Van Nguyen stood in the doorway of his mud-and-thatch hut, contemplating the sweltering heat of the early morning, and wishing that he didn't have to work the fields. Maybe just once he could sit around in the shade and watch the dark clouds build into rainstorms until the lightning flashed and the thunder roared. He wished his two sons hadn't run off in the night to join the Vietcong because, now that his fingers were bent with arthritis and his back hurt all the time, he needed them. He wished his daughters hadn't been drawn to Tay Ninh City by the lure of the American riches to be found there.

He glanced over his shoulder at his old wife, sitting in the darkness of the hut, sweat staining her light cotton shirt and dripping down her face. He wished she had the strength to help in the field, but the bombs that rained from the sky had crippled her long ago. He didn't know if they had come from the North Vietnamese, the South Vietnamese, the Vietcong or the Americans. All he knew was that she hadn't been the same since the day he'd found her lying in a puddle of blood among the new rice plants. She was unable to work in the fields and had trouble walking. The only thing she still did well was sleep.

Without a word to her, he left the hut. He wasn't even sure anymore that she heard him when he spoke to her. She stayed in the hut all day, and on many afternoons he was forced to carry water from the stream to bathe her because she didn't answer the calls of nature.

He picked up the shovel that he had found. It was a flat-bladed tool with a broken handle that the Americans had discarded. He had replaced the handle with a length of bamboo and wondered why anyone would throw away something so valuable, even if the handle was broken. It was the best thing to have happened to him in a year.

In the field he stripped off the black pajama shirt he wore so that he was bare to the waist. Not more than a half a kilometer away, another farmer was tending his crops. Nguyen waved at his friend who occupied a similar hut not far from his own. When the man responded, Nguyen bent to work, digging at a dike so that the water in the paddy behind it would flood into the dry one. It was time to get ready for the planting there.

Overhead, the American jets roared as they crisscrossed the skies from Thailand to the South China Sea in search of the enemy, many of them leaving spidery silk threads in the deep blue. There was the distant boom of artillery as it destroyed some other farmer's fields. And there was the rattle of small arms as the enemies tried to kill one another in a finger of jungle about a mile away.

Tan Van Nguyen tuned it all out. It wasn't his business. He didn't care who won the war, and in any case he couldn't tell which side was which. He only knew the misery that it had caused him. Sons who were missing, possibly never to be heard from again, and daughters who would never help him with their mother. They sometimes came home, bringing gifts of food and clothes and, once, a fancy fan that was useless because there was no electricity.

He tossed a final shovelful of stinking mud up onto the dike and climbed to the top of it as the foul-smelling water drained from one paddy into the other. He sat down, the shovel beside him, and watched the spreading stain of brown water, the sweat dripping from his nose and chin and down his neck to his chest. A hot, miserable day, just one of many that had preceded it and a harbinger of more to come.

It was then that he heard the distant, distinct pop of a mortar round being fired. He glanced up at his hut and saw the explosion as the round detonated. The black cloud of smoke and dust vanished in the light breeze as shrapnel ripped through the flimsy walls of his home.

For a moment he sat dumbfounded, too stunned to move or react. He watched as his life blew up in front of him. Mortars landed near the hut and in the water buffalo pen, wounding the beast. As it bellowed its rage and pain, two rounds dropped through the roof of the hut, blowing the top off and collapsing the front.

Tan Van Nguyen leaped to his feet and jumped into the muddy water. As he began running toward the smoking remains of his home, mortar rounds raining down around it, he saw the tiny well vanish in a puff of smoke. He heard the shout of a neighboring farmer and the scream of anguish that came from a nearby hut.

As the farmers neared the remains of their homes, the tree line that stood on the Cambodian border erupted into small-arms fire. The bullets sounded like angry bees, cutting down the wounded water buffalo and one of Tan Van Nguyen's neighbors. Then the black-clad men emerged from their cover, shooting their rifles from their hips and shouting for a long life for Ho Chi Minh and for the death of the imperialist running dogs from the West. Death to the puppet soldiers from Saigon and their evil spawn. Death to all who opposed them.

Tan Van Nguyen ignored the danger as he raced to his home. He slid to a halt near the rubble that had been the front. Inside, a single hand was visible. It was surrounded by a spreading pool of bright red, and he knew that his wife had finally been taken from him, too.

He turned and glared at the approaching soldiers. He yelled at them, demanding to know why. Why had they attacked him and the tiny hamlet where he lived? He and his wife, the people of the settlement, had done nothing to deserve the attack.

But that didn't stop the VC. They advanced rapidly, their weapons ripping at the mud walls that still stood, cutting down everything that moved. Nguyen saw a farmer break for the tree line, attempting to escape the burning thatch of his roof. He had taken no more than a few steps when he suddenly seemed to do a jerky dance, then his body sprawled in the dirt, bleeding from a dozen wounds.

Nguyen watched the death of his friend in horror and then realized that in order to survive he had to flee. He glanced at the hand of his dead wife one last time, then turned to run. As he sprinted across the open ground, bullets danced at his feet, and he felt the sting of a rock kicked up by a stray round. He dived for cover in a clump of trees, then began to crawl through it rapidly, the shouting and shooting diminishing in the distance behind him.

He would never return to the hamlet. Of that he was sure. Neither his sons, nor his daughters would come back now. Somehow they would learn of the destruction and would not return. They would forget about him and their mother. They would go on with their lives, forgetting about the tiny hamlet where they had been born and where they had grown up.

Without looking back, he headed north, thinking of the camp the Americans had built not far from the hamlet. A sudden sense of security swept over him as he thought of the Americans, tall, robust men who had promised to protect those who came to them. Nguyen had nothing now except the black shorts he wore. He decided he would go to the American camp and ask for their help.

Finally the heat overwhelmed him. He collapsed, breathing rapidly, his mouth full of cotton. He had nothing left, not even the shovel that had been thrown away. As he smelled the hot, dry dirt of his beloved Vietnam inches from his nose, he couldn't believe what had happened to him. He watched his sweat mingling with the reddish dirt, trying to understand why it had happened. There was no reason for the Vietcong to attack him or his hamlet. None whatsoever.

What he didn't know and couldn't be told was that the hamlet stood on an escape route. In the coming days and weeks, the NVA and VC would want a clear path into the Cambodian sanctuary, and it was Tan Van Nguyen's misfortune to have built his hut on one of the best escape routes.

1

THE ORIENTAL HOTEL
SAIGON, RVN

U.S. Army Special Forces Captain Mack Gerber sat in the air-conditioned luxury of one of the Oriental's bars and stared across the table at his companion. Gerber, possibly the most senior captain in the U.S. Army because he was on the promotion list for major, was a fairly young man for his rank. He was tall, just over six feet, with brown hair and blue eyes. His skin was a reddish-brown from so much time spent in the hot tropical sun. Until only a few weeks earlier, he had been in the World, teaching younger men what they should need to know to survive for their year in Vietnam. Now, on his second tour, he was assigned to MACV-SOG in Saigon. His assignment as the commander of B-52, a Special Forces operation in Nha Trang, had blown up with the company he had escorted into the Hobo Woods.

The woman with him, Robin Morrow, was a journalist assigned to a press bureau in Saigon. She was a young woman with light brown hair cut in bangs and bright green eyes. Unlike many of the journalists in the bar, she wasn't wearing fatigues or safari-style khakis. Instead, she was wearing a light, green silk dress that molded itself to her body. She wasn't watching Gerber, concentrating instead on the glass that held the tiny ice cubes and the almost nonexistent alcohol of her old-fashioned. She was spinning it so that the cubes rattled.

Finally she looked up. "Have you heard from my sister?"

Before he could answer, the waitress reappeared and took another drink order. Gerber waited until she vanished into the gloom before he spoke. "Heard from your sister? Well, yes, Robin, I have. Recently, in fact."

"And?"

"And," Gerber repeated. "And I haven't written back to her yet. With everything that's happened since I set foot in-country, I haven't had much in the way of spare time for writing letters."

"Uh-huh." Robin looked up and stared at Gerber. "I notice you're avoiding the question. I can only assume the worst."

Gerber picked up his empty glass, glanced at it as if seeing it for the first time, then set it down. "This isn't easy." He cleared his throat. Not as easy as facing the Vietcong over the sights of a rifle or waiting for the random mortar round to drop on him.

"I'm a big girl," said Robin. "You don't have to spare my feelings." She was quiet for a moment and then her voice hardened. "I can take anything but this beating around the bush, damn it. I have a right to know what's going on."

"Yeah." Gerber rubbed his face with both hands and wished the waitress would return with a fresh glass of bourbon. Hell, he wished she'd return with the bottle. "Robin, there's really not much to tell. The letter I got from her scolded me for my lack of sensitivity. She claims

I should have told her about the orders to Vietnam. But she understands now."

"Well, shit." Robin stared with total fascination at something on the ceiling, her eyes blinking rapidly to stop the tears. "Shit, shit, shit."

Gerber reached out and touched her hand. She drew it away from him. "Don't!"

"I'm handling this badly," he said. "You're misunderstanding everything here. Maybe it will help if I tell you that something has changed in the past year. I've had a chance to watch Karen carefully. . . ."

"That helps a great deal," snapped Robin. "I'm so happy that you had the opportunity to watch Karen carefully for the past year."

Gerber suddenly had a vision of Robin on the bar of a smoky club, a hundred GIs watching as she slowly stripped off her clothes, throwing them at him and flaunting herself while demanding that he watch. While the GIs had shouted encouragement and waved dollar bills at her, Gerber had felt sick to his stomach. He remembered the pain etched on her face as she'd stood outside the same club, Gerber's fatigue jacket around her to hide her nudity. The MPs had stood close, listening to them talk, but none of them had entered the conversation. They had just wanted to make sure that the scene wasn't going to get worse and that no one got hurt.

"What I'm trying to say is that I've seen her at her worst," Gerber finally said. "She tried to manipulate everything and everyone around her. Her world centers on her completely. She gets what she wants and then discards it because she knows she can do better if she tries."

"That's my sister," agreed Robin. "But no one seems to see it but me."

"The point," said Gerber, ignoring what Robin had said, "is that I left her high and dry. I didn't tell her about the impending trip to Vietnam because I didn't care what she felt. I didn't care about her. She'd taken our relationship and destroyed it."

Robin heard the words but couldn't believe them for a moment. She reached out now to touch Gerber, but then the waitress was there putting the drinks on the table, smiling broadly for a larger tip. Gerber handed her the money. When she left, Robin said, "She destroyed it?"

"I don't know how to say this without hurting you all over again, but I need to explain it. Karen and I'd go out to dinner, and she'd flirt with every man she saw. She's the center of her world, has to be the center of attention, and she thinks she's everyone's ideal of the perfect woman."

"Yes, that's my sister."

"Anyway, I realized she wasn't what I wanted." He stopped and smiled. "And I realized I wasn't what she wanted, either. At least I wouldn't be when I was captured again. As long as I was the one in control, as long as she had to pursue me, then she'd go to any lengths to catch me. Once that was done, I'd be discarded."

"I don't believe it." Robin shook her head. "Someone's actually seen through her." She took a healthy swig from her drink and made a face as the liquor burned her throat. "You should have heard my mother when Karen announced she was going into nursing. What a loving and caring person she was to devote her life to the service of others."

"A clever dodge," said Gerber, almost to himself. He picked up his glass but didn't drink. Instead he watched Robin as she talked.

"When I said I was going into journalism, she said it was so typical of me, always putting myself above everyone else. I told her it was a career of service as well, but she didn't see it that way."

Gerber felt his stomach flip at that. He could imagine the pain of a girl as her mother called her unfeeling, especially after she had praised her sister. He couldn't understand how parents could be so cruel, and yet he had seen it a hundred times. He had seen it in the faces of the young men who arrived at Fort Bragg for training. Not the draftees, but the young volunteers who were trying to do something so that the unfeeling men and women who masqueraded as their parents would notice them.

"The point of all this," said Gerber, "is that I broke it off with her. Ended it before the trip to Vietnam, in fact. I was the one who ended the relationship when I discovered what a carnivorous creature she was."

"Oh, my." Robin clapped her hands. "Oh, my! I bet she went into a frenzy."

"Doesn't matter. I saw her for what she really is. Love may be blind, but it isn't stupid. I saw her play a hundred other men, and a few women, like they were so many game fish. I didn't like it."

Robin leaned forward, her elbows on the table, the movement revealing more cleavage. She reached across and touched Gerber's hands, then released them immediately. She had felt the same electricity she always did when they touched. "So you're through with Karen?"

"Yes," said Gerber smiling. "She's there in the World, and in a year she'll have moved on to other things. Other people."

"Okay," said Robin, nodding. "Now we have to decide what we're going to do."

"You mean with our lives?"

"No, silly. With the rest of the night. I'm not hungry at all. A little drunk, but not hungry."

"I'd planned on dinner," said Gerber. "I haven't eaten since breakfast."

Robin was on her feet then, reaching for him. "We'll eat later." It was almost a command.

Gerber began to slide back his chair, when Robin collapsed into hers, her face suddenly white, as if an apparition had appeared in the doorway. Gerber turned to see Master Sergeant Anthony B. Fetterman approaching.

"Don't worry," he said to Robin. "This is probably nothing to worry about. He then turned to face Fetterman. The master sergeant was a diminutive man, wiry with black hair and dark eyes. He claimed various ancestry from the Sioux Indians to the Aztecs, and for his small size was the most deadly man Gerber had ever known. His skill at warfare was unmatched.

"Good evening, Tony," Gerber said.

Fetterman stopped and nodded at Robin. "Good to see you, Miss Morrow. You're looking especially pretty this evening."

"Thank you," she said, her voice quiet.

"Captain, I'm afraid I have some bad news."

Gerber nodded. "Spill it."

Fetterman looked at Morrow and smiled. "Sir, we've been asked to attend a briefing over at MACV Headquarters, due to start in the next few minutes."

"Now why aren't I at all surprised about that?" asked Gerber.

Fetterman ignored the question. "I'll meet you in the lobby. I appropriated us a jeep."

As Fetterman turned to leave, Gerber said, "I'm sorry, Robin. I've got to go."

She couldn't help smiling. "Somehow I knew this was going to happen. The evening was going too well. The gods don't want us to get too happy. It frightens them." She held up a hand to stave off his protest. "No, Mack, I understand. Call me when you get back, no matter what the time."

"You got it," he said. He reached out and touched her cheek, wishing he could kiss her, but not wanting to do it in the public bar. "I'll call."

He turned and hurried after Fetterman. Before he left the bar, he glanced back and saw her sitting quietly, a little smile on her face and her drink in her hands.

He found the master sergeant standing in the hotel lobby. Gerber followed his gaze, coming to rest on an American woman. Probably an employee at the embassy, he thought. She was small, with short dark hair. She wore a white blouse and a knee-length skirt, and when she turned she smiled at them, displaying perfect white teeth.

"Friend of yours?" asked Gerber.

"No, sir, but I sure wish she was."

"Where's this jeep of yours?"

Fetterman nodded toward the double glass doors. "On the street of course. Double-parked with the doorman watching it for me."

Together they crossed the marble-and-carpet expanse of the lobby. The clerk, standing behind a long desk, had his back turned and was shoving messages into the mail slots for the rooms.

As they passed through the doors, the heat and humidity of the tropical night washed over them like a wave on a beach. It was a physical assault. Even in the late evening the air was heavy with humidity.

Gerber stepped between two parked cars and climbed into the passenger side of the jeep. Fetterman walked around the front and got into the driver's seat. He twisted the ignition switch, turned on the lights, and then fought with the stick, shifting into gear.

He pulled out into the heavy traffic. Bicycles, Lambrettas, cars, jeeps and trucks inched along the roadway. The night was alive with people, all looking for something in the nightlife of South Vietnam's capital, while others walked along the streets, waiting for an opportunity to make some money.

From an alley came the driving beat of rock and roll that attempted to drown out the other night sounds. Standing in front of a neon-lit nightclub were half a dozen GIs and their dates, dancing and drinking on the sidewalk while a small knot of curious onlookers stood nearby.

Fetterman turned a corner, and the bustle was suddenly gone, replaced with the serenity of the wide palm-lined street that led past the presidential palace and a French cemetery. Gerber leaned back in his seat and put a foot up on the dashboard. The rush of air caused by the racing jeep dried the sweat from his face and cooled him. "I'll never get used to this," he shouted over the noise of the wind.

"Used to what?"

"Saigon. Christ, Tony, on one street you have whores chasing everyone and on the next you have a cemetery. The sound of traffic in the night, a horn, the roar of a souped-up motorcycle engine, and then the scream of rockets dropping into the crowd as jets fly overhead. It's all unreal."

Fetterman shot a glance at the captain and then made another turn, bringing them back into the honky-tonk of another neon-splashed street. Music drifted on the warm breeze. Then a woman screamed as if in abject terror. Fetterman slowed. They saw a soldier chasing a Vietnamese woman who screamed again and then stopped and fell, giggling, into the arms of the man. She obviously didn't need any help.

"Christ," said Gerber again.

And then they were away from that and into the outskirts of Saigon. In the distance Gerber saw the blaze of lights that marked the MACV Headquarters, making it a bright, visible target for enemy gunners who somehow refused to shoot at it. Maybe they felt that dropping mortars and rockets on the offices of the generals would result in a renewed, more vigorous campaign against them.

Fetterman turned into the parking lot and stopped near the white chain that marked the perimeter. He shut off the engine and then used a chain bolted to the floor of the jeep to lock the steering wheel in place. The chain and its padlock made it a little harder for thieves.

Together Gerber and Fetterman passed through the gate where a bored MP looked at them, saw that they were obviously Americans and waved them through without asking for ID cards. Fetterman opened the first of the double glass doors that led to the air-conditioned interior, and Gerber got the second one. They walked down the green-tiled floor that had been recently swept, along walls lined with posters that told soldiers to wear their ribbons proudly, to avoid spilling secrets to the enemy by remembering COMSEC and to ignore the local women who were probably disease-ridden and all whores anyway. It was the land of Army propaganda that threatened to ruin the war by turning it into a Madison Avenue campaign.

As they approached a set of stairs, Gerber asked, "Where is this boondoggle taking place?"

"Upstairs. Conference Room A-102."

They climbed to the second floor and entered another corridor. There were patches of light spilling into it from offices that were still occupied, even though most of the staff officers had left for the fun and adventure of downtown Saigon. Gerber stopped and read a few of the signs over the doors, surprised that offices that should be anonymous were clearly marked for enemy saboteurs if they happened to break into the building. It would be too bad if some general or colonel had to ask for help when he visited. Label everything so that it was easy to find.

Gerber wondered where his bad mood had developed. Maybe it was seeing the waste in downtown Saigon. Maybe it was the contrast between the poor and the rich, or the soldiers who had nothing better to do than chase the local women who were trying to earn a few dollars. Perhaps it was the MACV Headquarters, where the generals and colonels sat in air-conditioned comfort from nine to five, running the war when it was convenient for them. He wondered if it was the poster that cautioned the average soldier to protect classified material, and then labeling every door in the headquarters so that an enemy who gained access to the building would have no trouble finding those protected classified documents.

Fetterman halted in front of a closed door. "This is it." He knocked, and a voice from inside told them to enter.

The master sergeant opened the door and stood back
to let Gerber in. The captain glanced at the men sitting
around a highly polished conference table littered with
the remains of a late dinner. There were plates covered
with drying gravy and the remains of sandwiches and the
wrappings they had come in. Styrofoam cups stood half
filled. The ashtrays were overflowing with cigarette
butts, and the air in the room was blue with smoke.

"Come on in, Captain," said the man at the head of
the table. Unlike most of the others, he wore a khaki
uniform decorated with general's stars and rows of ribbons. He was a short burly man with thick wavy black
hair sprinkled with gray. His eyebrows were massive,
giving him a perpetual frown. "Come on in and have a
seat. We've just about figured out what you're going to
be doing for the next several days. I'm sure you'll find it
most educational and very interesting."

2

SPECIAL FORCES CAMP
A-337, PLEI SOI

LLDB Captain Minh crouched in the sandbagged fire control tower and surveyed the open ground around his camp. Minh was a Vietnamese officer who had come up through the ranks after attending the British military academy at Sandhurst, and who had earned his rank rather than having bought it.

Using binoculars stolen from the American Navy, he scanned the light brush and rice paddies to the south and west and the thicker jungle to the north, searching for the flash of mortar tubes. So far he hadn't been successful.

He dropped to the dirty floor made of heavy planking as three rounds detonated inside his camp. The first fell among the hootches used by the Vietnamese strikers as living quarters, doing little damage and injuring no one. The second exploded harmlessly on open ground behind the bunker line, and the third detonated outside the camp in the wire.

With the last explosion, Minh was on his feet again, but there was nothing more to be seen. He grabbed the field phone, the communications link to the command post almost directly under him, and blew twice into the mouthpiece. "Still nothing sighted. No evidence of movement near the camp."

Captain Roger Fulton, Minh's American counterpart, crouched in the entrance of the command post, watching from ground level. He held the handset of the field phone to his ear while scanning the fields around him. Fulton was on his first tour in Vietnam, having arrived nearly nine months earlier with his A-Detachment. They had been posted to the camp, only a klick or so from Cambodia, with orders to monitor the traffic on the Ho Chi Minh Trail.

Fulton was a big man, nearly six-five, and weighed almost 250 pounds. He was heavily muscled, and his forearms were bigger than some men's thighs. While in Vietnam he had been tanned deeply, and with his black hair he looked Hispanic. There were laugh lines around his eyes and mouth, which suggested a sense of humor, but he wasn't laughing now. He was worried about the mortar attack, because it was the fourth they had suffered in two days, and that suggested the enemy was up to something.

He glanced over his shoulder into the dimly lit recesses of the command post. "Have pits one and two throw some illumination up. Two rounds each and have them stand by," he ordered.

"Yes, sir," said Sergeant David Miller. Miller was a younger man and the senior communications NCO. He was lying on the floor behind the counter, the various radios and telephones near him. The heavily sandbagged command bunker was safe from everything except a direct hit by a rocket, but Miller wasn't taking any chances. He wore a flak jacket and steel pot and wished he had a suit of armor. He was too short to get killed now that he was a double-digit midget. He was due to rotate home in fewer than one hundred days.

He rolled to his right, grabbed the handset for the commo link with the mortar pits, then passed on Captain Fulton's instructions.

A moment later there was a dull pop and a flare blossomed over the camp, drifting slowly to the east, held aloft by its parachute and the heat from the burning magnesium. It was joined by another and then another.

Fulton leaped to his feet, tossed the handset away from him and sprinted around the bunker to the base of the ladder that led up into the fire control tower. As the flares burned, some of the flaming magnesium dropping away, he scrambled up the ladder, nearly colliding with Minh when he got to the top.

"Watch it, old boy," said Minh, his British accent more prominent now than it had been on his return from England years before.

"Still nothing?"

"Still nothing," said Minh. "I think they've built leantos in front of the tubes to conceal the flashes."

Fulton rubbed his chin, feeling the rough stubble that meant he'd have to shave soon. He put his binoculars to his eyes and began a slow scan. He hated mortar attacks. He wasn't scared of them, because they did so little damage. He hated them because he was forced to respond in some fashion, and that ate up time. Time that he could be using in a hundred more profitable ways.

Directly to the south were rice paddies, clumps of coconuts and palms that protected farmers' hootches, and open fields. To the west were more open fields, some tree lines and the Cambodian border. North, about a half klick away, were the beginnings of the triple-canopy jungle. An entire NVA division could hide in the jungle, and unless there were American ground troops in there looking for that division, it could go undetected for months.

"Tomorrow," said Fulton, "I think we need to get some patrols out to the north, Dai Uy."

"Yes," agreed Minh. "Two or three and have them out for several days. Charlie's getting too bold."

There was a sudden rattling of small arms. Rifles and machine guns on the bunker line. The muzzle-flashes of the weapons twinkled below them, the ruby-colored tracers dancing out and bouncing high into the sky. Rounds tumbled through the air and climbed into the night.

Minh was on the phone quickly, trying to raise the command bunker on that section of the line. "North wall, north wall, what's happening down there?"

One of the Vietnamese NCOs answered on the field phone. Behind his voice, Minh could hear the staccato bursts from the light machine guns.

"We have movement in the wire."

Minh relayed the message, and Fulton spun around. He braced his elbows on the sandbags and studied the darkened ground in front of him. The last of the flares burned out, and the light vanished as if someone had thrown a switch.

"More illumination," he growled.

Minh grinned to himself, thinking that Fulton was like Gerber in many ways. When Minh had served with Gerber at the old Triple Nickel, they'd often forgotten the charade of advisers. Gerber would give an order as if he commanded the camp. Now Fulton did the same.

Minh picked up the field phone and gave the instruction to be relayed to the mortar pits.

Again there was a pop overhead, and the ground was bathed in the eerie yellowish light of the flares as they oscillated under their parachutes. The shadows shifted and slid, but Fulton couldn't see anything other than the bottom of a fifty-five-gallon drum that they had set out as an aiming stake for the machine gunners and grenadiers.

Over his shoulder Fulton ordered, "Cease fire. I see nothing, no movement in the wire."

Minh relayed the order and then moved closer to Fulton. "You expecting trouble?"

"Not tonight," he said. "Not now. They've got us awake, but they haven't subjected us to a heavy bombardment yet. I think maybe two, three days before they hit us with any kind of concentrated ground assault."

Minh let his binoculars fall against his chest, held around his neck by a strap. "I'll call Saigon and let them know we're expecting trouble."

"I don't know about that," said Fulton. "Maybe you better let me contact my people in Nha Trang and see what they want to do. We don't want to give anything away to the VC."

Minh nodded, understanding that Fulton was afraid the VC, who had infiltrated the Vietnamese army and political structure, would get the warning before Minh's people did. Any help sent from Saigon would be riddled with VC and could prove to be more harmful than helpful.

"I doubt we'll have any more trouble for a while," added Fulton. "Half alert until midnight and then full alert. Maybe rotate the men in the LPs. Let's be ready in case the VC are being cute."

"I'll relay the orders to my men. I've already put my best men out in the listening posts, so they should be fine until morning," said Minh. "And you?"

"I'll be in the team house for about an hour and then I think I'll tour the bunker line. Just in case."

"Good," said Minh.

GERBER SLIPPED INTO A CHAIR at the table and waited. Fetterman stood for a moment and then sat down next to a major who held a fancy briefcase in his lap.

"All right," said the general. "Now that we're all here we can get this started." He turned, leaning back in his chair so he could pull the cover off the easel that stood behind him.

Under the cover was a large-scale map of a Special Forces camp situated close to the Cambodian border. It wasn't a typical camp. There were actually three separate compounds protected by a large network of wire and punji barricades. The entire camp, including the center redoubt where the American Special Forces men worked and slept, was surrounded by more wire, punji pits and booby traps.

"Major O'Herlihy, if you'll provide us with the current situation please."

"Thank you, General Davidson." O'Herlihy, a thin balding man with light eyebrows and a nose that was burned red and peeling badly, got to his feet. He moved to the front and took a pen from the pocket of his freshly cleaned, pressed jungle fatigues. He yanked on it, turning it into a pointer for use with the map.

"Gentlemen, this is Camp A-337 near the Cambodian border. It's always been a hot spot because Charlie can sit in Cambodia and lob shells and fire rockets into it without fear of retaliation by us."

Gerber interrupted. "But they've fired countermortar anyway?" It was a question.

O'Herlihy looked at Gerber. "When they've been able to spot the enemy tube, they've returned fire, even when it was sited on the opposite side of the border." O'Herlihy grinned sheepishly, as if he had just let a vital piece of information slip, and added hastily, "But that's not for discussion outside this room."

He looked at the faces of the men, and before continuing, consulted his notes. He flipped through several pages, then glanced at the general. "Now, in the past few weeks, we've been getting an indication of a buildup around the camp. Charlie, supported by the NVA, has been moving people and supplies into the general vicinity of the camp. There have been attacks by the NVA and VC on the small hamlets near Cambodia, as if to drive the locals from the area. Not the normal warnings that would cause them to leave, but actual attacks that force them to flee. One village was wiped out recently. Given all that, we believe the enemy is going to make a push to overrun the camp."

O'Herlihy hesitated, pausing long enough to get a reaction from the men in the room. When that didn't happen, he hurried on. "Given the location of the camp, we think it's in a very bad position."

With that, O'Herlihy went on to outline everything that had happened during the past few days, including the evidence of heavy enemy traffic detected by the infrared and heat-sensing equipment that had been planted along the border. He also detailed the evidence collected by the patrols, not only from that camp, but from the other military installations in the area. It was a long list of seemingly random items that when plotted on a map showed a plan behind the incidents. It was a coordinated effort.

When O'Herlihy resumed his seat, Gerber said, "This is the same kind of nonsense we've been picking up for the past several weeks. Charlie and the NVA are on the move all over South Vietnam, not just in this one little corner north of Tay Ninh City. We've had that fight in the Hobo Woods. We've seen an increase in the traffic on the Trail suggesting a buildup. This is one more sign that something big is about to erupt."

Davidson nodded his agreement. "But right now we don't want to participate in a fight."

Gerber felt white-hot anger flash through him. He wanted to leap to his feet and scream at these people, but he didn't move, knowing his reaction would do little except get him removed from the conference and possibly MACV-SOG. He clenched his teeth and consciously forced himself to relax. Almost calmly he said. "I don't think I understand."

"Captain," said the general, "I know you're aware of the political nature of the war. You can't read the newspapers or magazines and not be aware of it."

"Yes, sir," said Gerber, speaking because he felt he had to say something. Anything.

"Now we're not in a fight where the freedom of democracy in the United States is at stake. Hell, if South Vietnam fell, what would it mean to us? That a third-rate nation that's had a tradition of domination for hundreds of years would continue in that tradition. One segment of the population would be suppressing another segment. And if the Communists did take over, it would only mean that another Asian government's fallen and the threat is still twelve thousand miles from home."

"Sir," interrupted one of the colonels, "we'd also see several other countries in this region fall, not to mention the bloodbath that would surely take place as the Communists sought to eliminate all opposition."

Davidson waved a hand as if to dismiss the last few comments. "Doesn't matter if all of Asia goes Communist, at least not to the average man in the street in downtown Peoria. All he's concerned with is putting food on the table, watching TV and going bowling. A bunch of slopes twelve thousand miles away mean nothing to him."

"Granted," said another colonel.

"So what does all this mean? What does all this infiltration of enemy troops and supplies mean to that man in Peoria, worried about his rent check and the leaking oil pan? It means nothing to him until the news media gets on the air telling him that two or three hundred American boys died in this stinkhole."

Gerber lowered his gaze and saw a single cigarette burn, a thick black line wriggling like a worm across the table. He knew what was coming next.

"Captain Gerber," said the general, "I want you and Sergeant Fetterman to fly out to this camp and look it over. I want you to determine whether we can, A, hold it against the enemy buildup, and B, if we should. If you decide that it isn't worth the effort, I want you to make immediate plans to evacuate the troops and then tear it down, destroying everything that might be useful to the enemy."

"You sure about this, General?" asked Gerber.

"Sure about it? Yes. I want a solid evaluation and a rational decision made. What I don't want are pictures on the evening news of a burning, smoking camp with bodies in the wires and a list of fifteen or twenty Americans who died holding the damned place. It's not worth it.''

Gerber turned so that he could look at the general. His gaze drifted to the rows of ribbons that decorated the man's left breast pocket. There were victory medals for World War II and campaign medals and citations for bravery. This was a man who had fought through the roughest of wars and been decorated for his participation. He was a man who knew how the soldier in the field felt and what the soldier in the field believed. He wasn't the kind of chairborne commando that had been rising to command all too often in Vietnam. He was a man who knew the score. All of that was obvious from the rows of ribbons and the various skill badges he wore. Yet his instructions were as ridiculous as those given by other Saigon commanders.

Davidson raked a hand through his hair. "Is there a problem, Captain?"

"May I ask a question?" said Gerber.

The general glanced at the other men. "We're all friends here." He grinned as he said it.

"Then why don't we either make a commitment to make a stand at this camp or order the withdrawal now? Why send us out to look over the situation?"

"Good question," said Davidson. "Let's just say that I'm not happy with the intelligence we're getting. I want someone to look over the situation and render an assessment that I can live with, someone whose opinion will be more informed than that of a big-assed staff officer from Saigon. It's your call, either way, but I don't want a major battle developing over that camp. If Charlie is going to attack it in force, I want it abandoned and destroyed before that attack can take place. This isn't the right time for a full-scale battle."

Gerber looked back at Sergeant Fetterman. "Tony, you have any questions?"

"Yes, sir. Just one. Why in hell are we working so hard to avoid a fight with the enemy? I thought that's what we were here for in the first place."

The meeting broke up thirty minutes later, with Fetterman's question still unanswered. Instead, each man provided some direction for the evaluation and let it go at that. The general then told Fetterman and Gerber that transportation would be available for them at Hotel Three at seven the next morning. He expected a report by three that same afternoon, not a final determination, but some kind of preliminary analysis.

With that, they left. When they reached the jeep, Fetterman climbed into the driver's side, unlocked the wheel and started the engine. For a moment he sat staring into the dark night and then asked, "You interested in a beer?"

Gerber shook his head, thinking of Robin Morrow waiting for him at the hotel, and then changed his mind. "Yeah, I do want one. Hell, I'll even buy."

"You have a preference as to the place?"

"Lead on, Tony. I'll trust your judgment."

Fetterman backed the jeep out and turned around. He drove to downtown Saigon, avoiding the dark streets because he was worried about snipers, and stopped in front of a bar with blaring music. There was an MP jeep parked in front of him. One of the men, his black helmet liner reflecting the bright lights, sat there watching the crowd.

Fetterman locked his jeep again and climbed out. He stood on the street, watching the young GIs dance with the local girls. Their party, though noisy, seemed tame enough.

Fetterman led Gerber into the smoke-filled bar, which was rocking with music. The walls seemed to vibrate. A single strobe flashed on the stage where a four-piece band belted out the latest rock hit with little enthusiasm and a girl wearing next to nothing danced to music that only she could hear.

The place was jammed with shouting, dancing, singing soldiers who were drinking beer as fast as they could, while others were throwing up on the floor. Two were slumped against the wall, a beer held in each hand as they slept.

"Nice place," shouted Gerber, not sure that Fetterman could hear him.

The master sergeant shouldered his way to the bar, managed to get two bottles of beer, then pushed his way clear. He handed one to Gerber, nodding in the direction of the door, but was intercepted by a huge black man who looked like an off-duty GI earning a little extra money as the bouncer. Fetterman handed the man some money and then escaped into the night where the temperature was at least thirty degrees cooler, hugging the low eighties.

Once they were outside, Gerber wasn't sure he'd ever be able to hear again. "What was that all about?"

"Bottle, sir. They can't get new bottles, and they're so afraid of losing one that they watch them carefully. Guy didn't want me to take it out. I told him we'd bring them back and then gave him five bucks."

Gerber took a drink and wanted to spit it out. It was the worst beer he had ever tasted. Fetterman, however, took a sip like a connoisseur tasting fine wine. He grinned at Gerber. "Ah, Tiger Piss. Aptly named."

"Tony, we could have gotten a good beer at the hotel. American beer or German beer. Anything but Vietnamese beer. For Christ's sake, Tony."

"Yes, sir, and chanced running into Miss Morrow or one of her reporter cronies."

"I'm not convinced running into Miss Morrow would be so bad, unless you have something you want to talk about?"

Fetterman moved back so that he could lean against the jeep. He took a drink. "Yes, sir. I'm getting a little tired of us avoiding a fight all the time. That seems to be the rule now. It's as if the brass sees the war as a good thing. Full employment, lots of promotions and good money. Us enlisted pukes don't have to pay income tax and you officer types get a big tax discount. It seems they believe that by fighting, we're going to screw up a good thing."

Gerber took another pull at the beer and felt like spitting again. He agreed with Fetterman. "You have a point here?"

"Suppose we get out there and find Charlie planning a big push on the camp. Now our orders are clear. We order everyone off the camp and destroy it. Again we go running from a fight."

"That's about it."

"So what if we don't find Charlie, and when they start storming the wire we say, 'Well, hell, General, the buildup must have been in Cambodia where we couldn't see it. They caught us all by surprise.'"

Gerber finished the beer and set the bottle on the hood of the jeep. He watched a soldier guide his date toward a shadow and then slide his hand inside her blouse. As he watched, he saw that the hand was a diversion, getting her attention while the other worked on the zipper of her skirt.

"You want to lie to the brass?"

"No, sir. I want to seek out the enemy. We know he's running around that camp. The evidence is there if those paper pushers want to see it. I'm just saying that we delay long enough for the enemy to hit the camp and then we'll have to defend it or get killed."

Gerber hopped up on the fender of the jeep and studied the dirty cigarette-studded sidewalk. "You know, Tony, you're always coming up with these wild-ass ideas that could get my ass in a sling. I seem to remember it was you who stumbled into that mess in the Hobo Woods while we were under orders not to engage in a full fight."

"Yes, sir, but it didn't turn out all that bad."

"Colonel Bates might not agree with that."

Fetterman shrugged. "The colonel didn't get into that much trouble. Hell, he's in Okinawa."

"But his name isn't on the list for general and might never be," said Gerber. "That's pretty stiff for someone who has made a career out of the military. Finishes his career just short of his ultimate goal."

"I'm sorry about that, but the colonel went along with us. Besides, after a couple of months, he might find himself on the list again."

Gerber shook his head. "Don't be so sure. You don't understand about those ringknockers. One of them doesn't like you, they all don't like you. A ringknocker wants to destroy you, he can usually do it."

"So you're saying we're not going to pursue this. We go out and find the enemy and close the camp."

"Now what in hell could I have said to give you that impression? I was only explaining the facts of life to you. Tomorrow we go check the situation, and if we can pull it off, we stay right there and let Charlie beat his brains out trying to overrun the damn place.''

Fetterman clapped his hands together. ''All right, Captain. That's what I wanted to hear. I tell you what, I'll buy us another beer apiece to celebrate.''

''Does it have to be Tiger Piss? Can't we just go over to the hotel and get a real one?''

''Thought you liked to indulge yourself once in a while by seeing how the other half lives. Come down and wallow in the slime with the rest of the enlisted pukes.''

''No, Tony. That's not something I've ever said. Now let's get over to the hotel and I'll buy the beer. But only one.''

''Yeah,'' he said, grinning. ''Don't want to keep Miss Morrow waiting too long.''

''Shut up, Master Sergeant. Just shut up.''

3

HOTEL THREE, TAN SON NHUT, SAIGON

Gerber stood in the terminal building housed underneath the control tower of Hotel Three and watched the rain coming down in heavy sheets. It was a freak storm, which, when it came up during the dry season, washed out roads and rice paddy dikes and destroyed mud-walled hootches and water buffalo pens. It was a rain that came down with a vengeance, striking the ground and bouncing high and even here, away from the jungle, it sounded like frying bacon.

At his feet, away from the door and the rain, was his rucksack. There wasn't much in it except for clean clothes and a shaving kit. Gerber didn't expect to be in the field, and anything he needed other than his personal items could be obtained at the Special Forces camp. He also had a pistol belt, which held two canteens, a small first-aid kit and a holster with a Browning M-35 pistol.

A shape materialized out of the grayness of the rain and rushed the door. Fetterman appeared, the rainwater having soaked his uniform, turning it from OD green to black. He dropped his rucksack on the dirty concrete floor of the terminal and turned to look back the way he had come.

"Christ, it's a fucking monsoon out there. I can't even see the gate."

Gerber moved closer. "It's not a monsoon. Not yet anyway."

Fetterman unslung his weapon from across his shoulder and turned it upside down, pouring the rainwater from the barrel. "I hope we don't find ourselves in a firefight before I get a chance to clean this."

"Where in hell did you get that thing?" asked Gerber. He reached out and touched the weapon, an old M-3 grease gun. The Army had declared it obsolete in 1957, and every time Fetterman showed up he had one. It was as if the master sergeant had a secret supply of them somewhere, close.

Fetterman held it out as if he had seen it for the first time. "This?" Now he smiled slyly. "Well, we NCOs can find anything we want. This is a good weapon. It fires .45-caliber ammo, which means finding ammo isn't a problem, and the cyclic rate of fire is slow enough that it doesn't burn through the rounds the way the M-16 and M-60 do."

"Sergeant, I didn't ask for a weapons class. I asked where in hell you keep getting all these M-3s? That can't be the same one you had on our last tour."

"No, sir. That one's gone, but more of them are around, if you know where to look. Got this from a friend over in the Twenty-fifth Infantry Division. If you'd like one, sir, I can probably scare up another." He ignored the fact that there were a few SF weapons rooms around loaded with old, reliable and now sterile weapons.

Gerber shook his head. "No, thanks anyway."

"Doesn't look like we're going to be flying out to anywhere for a while," said Fetterman, studying the rain.

"Yeah," agreed Gerber. He turned and moved toward the counter where a bored sergeant sat reading a paperback novel. "Any coffee available?" he asked the man.

"Pot over there. Help yourself."

"Tony? Coffee?"

"No, thanks."

Gerber poured himself a cup and then dropped a lump of sugar into it. Normally he refused the sugar, but he didn't know how long the coffee had been brewing and was afraid it would be like so much else in the Army—ruined by people who had no idea what they were doing, but were out there doing it as fast as they could anyway.

Gerber stirred the coffee, thinking about the night before, after Fetterman had dropped him off at the hotel. As the master sergeant had driven off toward his quarters in the Tan Son Nhut, Gerber had gone upstairs. He had planned to call Robin and tell her that he wouldn't be able to meet her that night, but when he'd entered his room, he'd found that she'd let herself in.

Staring out the lightly fogged window of the terminal, Gerber remembered the sight vividly. Robin had been sitting on the bed, her back against the wall and a magazine in her lap. Her green silk dress had been folded neatly and set on the chair. She was wearing only panties, a garter belt and stockings. She turned and smiled as he entered. "What kept you?"

Gerber rubbed his face and stared. Then he turned and locked the door. "You've been waiting?"

She put the magazine aside. "Why wouldn't I?"

"Well, I might not have come back. You know how these Army missions work."

"Then I would have finally turned off the light and gone to sleep."

Gerber entered the room and sat down. With his eyes on Morrow, he untied his boots. He kicked them off, rubbed his feet, then stretched. He smiled at Morrow, thinking that she was not only smart, but she was good-looking. Her light blond hair framed her face. The light reflected from her sweat-damp skin.

Morrow got to her feet and moved to Gerber. She stepped behind him and rubbed his shoulders. "Relax," she said. "Just relax. We have all the time in the world."

Gerber grabbed her hand and kissed her palm. "I'm afraid we've only got a few hours."

She moved around in front of him and knelt, one hand on his knee. "A few hours?"

"Don't look so devastated. I'm only going out to one of the SF camps for a couple of days."

She reached up and began unbuttoning his jungle jacket. She pulled it open and rubbed his chest. "Only a few days, huh? I've heard that before." She stood and pulled at him. "Come on, Mack. You have to cooperate."

"What do you want me to do?"

"First, I think you should shower and shave...."

"You telling me that I smell bad?" asked Gerber, grinning.

"No, I'm telling you that I think we should take a shower. And then turn off the air conditioner, and open the window."

Gerber looked past her at the window where the air conditioner hummed. "It's hot out there."

"Yes, but we have the ceiling fan. That'll keep us cool. It'll be romantic. Love in the tropics."

Gerber shook his head. "Okay, Robin. Whatever you want."

Afterward he had to admit that it had been interesting: both of them in a light coating of sweat that made their bodies slippery. That somehow heightened the sensuality of the moment. Everything was so smooth and light.

Gerber shook himself, driving the thoughts from his mind. With the mission coming up, the last thing he needed was to be thinking about Robin and the night before. He returned to the door where Fetterman was still watching the rain. Gerber sipped the coffee, little better than a cup of mud. "Looks like it's letting up."

"Some."

The gray clouds had lifted slightly, and the lights on the PX across from the tower and terminal, just behind the chain-link fence, were becoming visible. They created halos of colored light that suggested all of Tan Son Nhut hadn't washed away in the monsoon.

"The thing I don't like about the rain in the tropics," said Fetterman, "is that it never cools things off. It makes it worse. You've got the humidity to contend with." He wiped a hand over his forehead, soaking up the sweat that was beginning to bead there.

The rain slowed, and they saw that the airfield had survived the deluge. There was a roar of jet engines as a fighter took off to the west. Minutes later the popping of rotors indicated the approach of a helicopter.

"Bet that's our ride," said Fetterman.

Gerber drained his coffee, crushed the Styrofoam cup and tossed it at the wastebasket near the stained and ragged settee that neither had bothered with. A low table covered with tattered magazines sat in front of it.

A moment later they saw the vague outline of the chopper in the gray mist that hung over the airfield, its navigation lights flashing red and green. They were bright points in the mist that drew attention to the barely visible hulking machine.

Fetterman grabbed his gear and moved to the door. Gerber waited until the helicopter touched the ground and then did the same. Both of them ran through the mist, splashing through the puddles. Fetterman tossed his gear into the cargo compartment, then grabbed the hand offered by one of the crewmen. As Gerber climbed up after him, the chopper picked up to a hover, whipping the mist into circular patterns that slashed the ground and blew the puddles away from the aircraft.

They climbed out through the grayness and into the blackness of the storm clouds. Wind buffeted the chopper, throwing them about, and then they were away from it, into clear, bright sky to the west of Tan Son Nhut. In front of them there was nothing but blue sky while behind them the dark grays and blacks of the squall line massed.

They continued on, climbing to fifteen hundred feet, an altitude the pilots considered safe since it was outside of effective small-arms range. Gerber sat back on the red canvas troop seat and rested his head on the gray soundproofing around the transmission. Outside the cargo compartment doors were the bright greens of the trees and fields of South Vietnam. The colors seemed brighter in the early-morning sun, the dust and dirt having been washed from them by the recent storm.

Below them was Highway One, a road that led from the Vietnamese capital to Go Dau Ha, where the bridge spanning the Song Vam Co Dong was down more often than it was up. They stayed north of the highway and south of the major American base at Cu Chi that dwarfed the town. There was a single runway pointed almost north and south, with the traffic taking off to the north.

Once past it, they turned northwest, crossing the Hobo Woods. They were south of the Iron Triangle and approaching War Zone C. That was the stuff newscasts were made of, Gerber thought. These were the names that evoked some kind of image in the mind of the viewer. The Iron Triangle. War Zone C. It made it sound as if the war was being fought, while Gerber knew that it was being avoided as much as possible because they didn't want announcements on the six o'clock news that still another American boy had died in the fighting.

Gerber forced himself to relax, but it was difficult. He didn't like what was going on around him. Too often the press reports he read in *Time* and *Newsweek* had no relation to the events in Vietnam. Somehow, by the time the story got back to the World, it had been distorted. Then the brass in Vietnam, reacting to the negative press, made some ridiculous change causing more grief for the men in the field, but that looked good on paper.

He shook his head, trying to force the thoughts from his mind. At some point, he knew, they were all going to end up in a big fight. The VC and NVA were planning a major operation, and the fact that the brass and the press were ignoring the signs didn't mean it was going to go away.

Fetterman leaned close to shout over the roar of the Huey's engine, the pop of the rotors and the howl of the wind through the cargo compartment doors. "At least we won't be humping through the boondocks."

Gerber turned and stared at the master sergeant, unsure of what he was talking about.

"After the storm, with the humidity, at least we don't have to hump," said Fetterman, explaining.

"Yeah," said Gerber.

But that wasn't what he was concerned about. He was worried about what the general had said the night before. They were to look over the situation and decide whether or not the camp should stay open. It was the same fight he'd been involved in during his first tour: a constant war with the brass to keep his camp open because the enemy mortared and attacked it on a regular basis. When the enemy did that, it meant a camp was a sore point with them. Gerber remembered a number of fact-finding tours visiting the old Triple Nickel—officers dispatched from Saigon with orders to find out what was going on. None of those men on the fact-finding tours had understood the situation and each had suggested the camp would probably be better someplace else where the enemy wasn't quite as numerous.

That was exactly the instruction he had been given: look over the camp, with the implication that he should declare that it was in a bad location. Every time the brass learned that a camp was a thorn in the enemy's side, the immediate reaction was to move it somewhere else. Given everything that had happened in the past few weeks, maybe Fetterman was right. Maybe they should just hang around until things began to pop and then claim it was too late for them to do anything.

He leaned to the right. "I think the first thing to do is for you to get a patrol together and check out the terrain surrounding the camp."

"Looking for what?"

"The enemy. Signs that Charlie is in the region in force. See if you can spot a buildup around the camp that would suggest it's going to be attacked. While you're doing that, I'll talk to the team commander, this Captain Fulton, and see what his impressions are."

Fetterman had to smile. "You're getting even for that remark about not humping through the boonies, aren't you?"

"No. But I am getting even for your speech last night. I want to make a real assessment of what's happening at that camp. I want us to know by nightfall so that we can take steps to defend it. Then we beat around the bush until we have an opportunity to hurt the enemy."

"Yes, sir."

"Do you know anyone out there? I don't remember having ever seen this Fulton."

"I think there's a sergeant on the team I've met before. Sergeant Lopez. If it's the same guy, he'll be able to give us an accurate reading of the situation."

"I wish we had Kepler here," said Gerber. He laughed, thinking about the intel NCO on his former team, a man who had shown up at the camp dressed as a nurse and as a Navy lieutenant commander. Kepler would have been able to check out the countryside and tell them what was happening.

"Eleven Fingers is still in the World, I believe," said Fetterman.

"When we get back to Saigon, maybe we should request his presence here. Piss him off royally, but give us one more good man."

"Yes, sir," agreed Fetterman.

Gerber glanced to the right through the cargo compartment doors and saw the precise pattern of the rubber tree plantations east and north of Dau Tieng. There was the Saigon River to the north and that meant they were getting closer to Camp A-337.

They banked left, heading almost toward Nui Ba Den, the Black Virgin Mountain, then skirted the northern side of it, missing completely the huge American camp west of Tay Ninh City.

When they approached the Cambodian border, they began losing altitude as the pilot started a slow let-down, opting to low-level into the Special Forces camp to avoid the antiaircraft defenses erected on the border by the North Vietnamese.

Now they were screaming across the ground, dodging bushes and climbing to avoid rice paddy dikes and water buffalo. The air had changed from cool and dry air to warm and moist. The breeze blowing in the open doors of the cargo compartment was no longer comfortable. Gerber felt sweat pop out on his face and drip down his sides. Somehow the air had become heavy and oppressive.

Then, in the distance, through the windshield of the chopper, he could see a red slash in the green of the vegetation. Open rice paddies, reflecting the morning sun, were spread out almost like a blanket for a picnic. Farther north was the beginning of the central highlands and triple-canopy jungle. And nestled between the two extremes was Camp A-337, a sore that marked the American presence near Cambodia.

The chopper banked, dropped and raced along the ground, the skids barely above the tops of the rice plants in the paddies. They banked again, rolling up on the side so that it seemed the rotor blade would splinter against the ground. Then suddenly they righted themselves and the nose came up. Gerber felt his stomach flutter and then pressure on his body as the force of gravity increased, pushing down on the troop seat. There was a moment when it seemed the helicopter was going to be ripped apart by the various pressures and forces, and then the skids were on the ground.

The pilot turned in his seat and grinned at Gerber and Fetterman, flipping them a thumbs-up.

"Quite a ride!" shouted Fetterman, a wide smile on his face. "Quite a ride."

Gerber slid across the troop seat and dropped to the ground. He blinked in the bright sun, which seemed brighter after the rain had washed the air. He dragged some of his equipment across the floor of the cargo compartment and shouldered it. Fetterman jumped to the ground beside him, and as they moved off the landing pad, they were pushed forward by a sudden rush of hurricanelike wind.

The helicopter picked up to a hover and lifted off in a roar of engine noise and a whirlwind of swirling dirt and debris. In seconds it was little more than a speck on the horizon, the sound of the engine lost in the distance. Then it became quiet. There wasn't even the buzz of insects, the chirp of birds or the chattering of animals. For an instant, Gerber and Fetterman felt as if they had gone deaf.

Fetterman, speaking louder than normal, asked, "Shouldn't they be out here to meet us?"

As if in answer to his question, they heard the rumble of a truck as it exited the camp and turned toward them. It stopped short of them, and a big man in jungle fatigues dropped to the ground.

"Welcome," he said. "I'm Sergeant Paul Timmons, the heavy weapons man."

Gerber moved to shake hands with him. He noticed that Timmons had been made from the same mold as

Sam Anderson, one of his men who had been killed in action. Timmons was a huge Nordic man with light-colored hair and skin that seemed to be permanently sunburned. Looking about twenty-five, he had light blue eyes and a long nose and seemed ready to burst out laughing.

"Sorry we weren't out here to meet you, but you know how it is. Everyone suddenly has something else to do when the brass from Saigon arrives. They all want a chance to look you over before they have to come out and meet you. I'm not sure what they're afraid of."

Fetterman pushed forward and shook hands with Timmons. He grinned at the huge man. "I don't think of myself as the brass from Saigon. Hell, man, we're just here to look around for a couple of days. Nothing to it."

"Well, that's not the word we got from Saigon. We're supposed to be on good behavior or we'll find ourselves in deep shit."

"Then you'd think your detachment commander or the camp commander would have greeted us," said Gerber. "They're not making a very favorable impression."

"Yes, sir," agreed Timmons. He suppressed a smile and added, "But you know how officers are."

"Why don't you take us into the camp?" suggested Gerber.

Timmons spun around and walked to the back of the truck. "Toss your gear in there and climb aboard."

"Let's just walk it," said Gerber.

"Okay," said Timmons. "I'll have someone else come out and collect the truck."

They moved from the pad, a rubberized mat held down by a row of green sandbags along each corner, to the short grass of the open field. They reached a road of crushed gravel that led from the runway into the main camp, which looked like a concave box. Each of the walls was bowed inward slightly so that the corners on each side stuck out into the fields and the machine guns that were emplaced there could set up a cross fire regardless of the direction of the attack. There was a low bunker line protecting each of the walls, the firing slits only inches above the grass. The ground in front of the slits dropped away sharply to create moats that were filled with punji stakes.

They entered the compound through a flimsy gate made from two-by-fours and barbed wire. To the right, Gerber could see a number of Vietnamese working to shore up a bunker's wall. They were passing sandbags to one another but didn't seem to have any idea what they were doing.

The camp was a copy of a dozen others he had been in. Bunkers housing crew-served weapons and support machine guns guarded the interior. There were six strands of wire that contained booby traps, claymore mines and trip flares. If the enemy managed to penetrate both the wire and the bunker line, there was a secondary line of defense inside the redoubt. Each of the Vietnamese areas inside the main camp was constructed so that they could be used as secondary defenses. Clustered around the redoubt were the commo bunker, the command post and the fire control tower. Inside the redoubt were the team house, dispensary and the American quarters.

Sergeant Timmons walked past the bunkers, the line of men working and into the redoubt. He headed to the team house and opened the door, letting Gerber and Fetterman enter before him. It was like all the other team houses he'd seen: tables and chairs for the men and a bar behind which worked a single Vietnamese woman preparing the morning meal. They were always there making meals. And behind her were the stove, a refrigerator and a wall of canned goods, the latter purchased during the PX runs.

Timmons pointed to a table. "Have a seat. I'll see if I can find someone with some spare time. There's coffee in the pot if you feel like it."

After Timmons left, Fetterman asked, "Did I miss something, or are these people being deliberately rude?"

"I don't think they'd be deliberately rude, but then I don't know what the radio traffic might have been. Some joker in Saigon might have said something that pissed them off."

"Well," said Fetterman, "I don't like it. You'd think they'd at least wait to see what we had to say before acting like we had leprosy."

At that moment the door flew open, crashing into the wall behind it. But there was no one there, just a bright rectangle of light. Gerber stared at it, waiting for something to happen.

A figure centered itself in the door, and a voice asked, "I say, old boy, aren't you talking to your old friends?"

"Minh?"

"That's right."

Fetterman was on his feet, moving forward. "Captain Minh. Good to see you, sir. How have you been?"

Minh pulled a chair out and dropped into it. "I've been fine. Just fine." Minh was a small, slender man with black hair and dark eyes. There was a scar on his face from his left ear to his chin, a new scar that hadn't been there when either Gerber or Fetterman had last seen the man.

Minh looked uneasily from one American to the other. "When Captain Fulton found out I knew you, he sent me over to learn what was going on. He's most upset by this development."

"Yes," said Gerber, "I imagine he is, but you can tell him not to worry. Tony and I are here to look around and to determine whether the camp should be left where it is. The brass thinks another location for it might be more advantageous."

"Seems that was the argument used against the old Triple Nickel," said Minh.

"We thought so, too," said Fetterman. "Hell, you can tell the captain we're not here to cause him any grief. No one suggested the problems here are his fault."

"Are there problems here?" asked Gerber.

Minh shook his head, looking first at Gerber and then at Fetterman. "No more than we had at the Triple Nickel. Mortars every night, sometimes two or three at times. And our patrols are beginning to pick up evidence of more enemy in the vicinity. We think there's a push coming."

"Can you handle it?" asked Gerber.

"This is a good camp. Good men. We've had time to prepare it the way it should be done with a full complement of heavy weapons. It would take two, maybe three regiments to overrun us, and that's providing we couldn't get the air or artillery support that's available to us. Or that we couldn't get a Mike Force lifted in here."

"Tony?" said Gerber.

"If you don't mind, I'd like to go out with a patrol as you suggested. Look around for myself," Fetterman said.

"We've got a couple of short patrols going out at noon. You can join one of them if you like."

"That'll be fine."

"Now," said Gerber, "where's your counterpart?"

"Waiting for me to soften you up. He's convinced that anyone sent out from Saigon, regardless of the background, won't understand what's happening here."

At that moment Fulton stepped into the team house. He stopped and waited. Gerber stood and waved him over, holding out a hand. "Captain Fulton, I'm Captain Gerber."

"Captain."

"And this is Master Sergeant Fetterman."

When they had shaken hands all around and sat down, Fulton waved to the Vietnamese woman. "Trin," he called. As she came around the end of the bar, Fulton asked, "Coffee okay for everyone?"

"I'd prefer a glass of orange juice, if you can manage that," said Fetterman.

"We've got orange juice, but I'm afraid it's powdered and came in a paper sack. It probably tastes like cardboard dissolved in water."

"As long as it's cold, or cool at the least," said Fetterman.

Fulton gave the order to the woman, then turned back to Gerber. "I trust Dai Uy Minh filled you in on our situation."

"Yes," said Gerber, "but I don't think you understand our position." He saw the look on Fulton's face change to one of apprehension. He chuckled and added, "Captain, I was an A-Detachment commander on my first tour. I understand your trouble, but we've got to look around. We're not here to hang your ass, but to evaluate the situation."

"Sure."

Gerber looked at Minh. "Is he always this optimistic, or has someone just given him some good news?"

"I rather suspect, old boy, that he's gotten some good news recently."

"Captain," said Fetterman, "I'd like a chance to meet with the other team members, especially if I'm going out on patrol with them."

"Of course," said Fulton.

Gerber saw the Vietnamese woman returning. "Have your juice and then we'll get started."

4

THE HOTEL DOWNTOWN
SAIGON

Robin Morrow awoke for the second time about ten o'clock. The room was stifling, and both she and the sheets were soaked with sweat. She got out of bed and turned on the air conditioner, standing in front of it and letting it cool her. When the sweat had dried, she moved to the bathroom and turned on the water for a shower. She stepped into it, washed her body and then got out, drying herself with the huge hotel towels.

Once dressed, in the same clothes she'd worn the night before, she left the room and the hotel. She returned to her own room and went up to change. Then, wearing a khaki jumpsuit with the legs cut off at midthigh and the sleeves hacked off at the elbow, she left again. She carried her camera bag with her. In the lobby she thought about taking a cab, but as she moved through the glass doors to the sidewalk, she decided she didn't want to trust fate. She decided she would walk.

As she made her way along the streets of Saigon, she was assaulted by sound. Saigon wasn't a quiet city. There was the constant insectlike buzz of tiny Honda engines.

There was the backfiring of diesel-powered cars and trucks, drivers leaning on their horns, shouts and curses. Then there were the normal sounds of a city: people yelling at one another, music from bars that opened early and music from radios with the volume turned high. People were dickering and arguing and fighting. And over all that noise were the sounds of war. Jet aircraft overhead. Fighters and bombers and commercial planes. There were helicopters, some of them alone, and some in flights of five or ten. Each added its own noise to the din.

At the corner she stopped and held a hand to her eyes. Across the wide street crawling with cars, bicycles and motorcycles was a wide lawn that led to the presidential palace. It was surrounded by a high fence and patrolled by armed guards. At the gate two American MPs sat in a jeep with a machine gun mounted in the back.

Morrow crossed the street and thought about taking a picture of the MPs but decided there were already enough pictures of MPs sitting in jeeps in Saigon. Instead, she turned and hurried down the street to the Bureau offices of the wire service.

The building was a white three-story structure with the windows on the bottom floor boarded up. Morrow reached the door, knocked and waited until she heard a buzz that meant something had deactivated the lock from the inside. She stepped in, assaulted by the cold air. It was a physical blow after the heat and humidity of the streets. For a moment she stood there shivering, letting her body adjust to the difference in temperature. Finally she ran up the stairs, taking them two at a time.

At the top she stopped and hesitated. To the right was a hallway that led to the offices of the various correspondents. They were no more than cubicles, which contained desks and typewriters and anything else the correspondent could steal. In the other direction was the city room, if it could be called that. An open area the size of a barn and filled with desks, typewriters, tables and files, it was where most of the people worked.

Robin shrugged and turned left. She entered the city room, dropped her camera bag by the door and walked to the desk that was assigned to her. On it she found several message slips, all from sources in Saigon and not one from Gerber. She shrugged with disappointment and fell into her chair.

She sat quietly, flipping through the messages again and then dropped them on her desk. She rocked back in her chair and put her feet up, crossing her ankles. Slowly she surveyed the room.

Two walls were lined with large windows that let in all the tropical sun, creating a glare. There were blinds over the windows, but they were open. Those with the most seniority got the newer desks near the windows so that they could daydream while watching the population below them. Deeper in the room were the older desks, many of them scrounged from the military and painted a terrible shade of gray. Robin's desk was unusual because someone had found a spare can of paint and tried to cover the gray. The color that resulted was hard to define; it looked like a washed-out green.

One wall opposite the windows contained a number of small offices that belonged to the men and women who were only slightly less important than the correspondents. Along the other wall were file cabinets filled with information—everything anyone could possibly want to know about Saigon nightlife but little of any real importance.

From one of the offices a man emerged, searched the room and then spotted Morrow. He grinned and came toward her. "Late night?"

"Or early morning. Anything interesting happening?"

The newcomer, a slightly overweight short man with black hair and pasty skin, pulled a chair around so that he could sit. With his index finger he scratched his forehead. "Nothing. You'd think a war would be interesting all the time, but not this one."

Morrow dropped her feet to the floor and picked up her messages. "Got something here from MACV. A Major Dawson. You know anything about that?"

"Yeah. Dawson just received his ninth air medal. Claims he has more medals than anyone in Vietnam now and thought we'd like the story."

"Could be something," said Morrow.

"No. He's counting five good conduct medals he got when he was a sergeant, and a bunch of Army commendation medals. Highest thing he's got is a Bronze Star. It's nothing."

Morrow wadded up the slip and tossed it at the wastebasket, missing by a few inches.

"Your captain up to anything?" he asked.

"You heard something, Mark?"

"No. Not a thing. I just thought that since he's in the Green Berets he might have a line on something. Anything."

Morrow looked at the nearly empty room. "Is it as bad as all that? Where the hell is everyone?"

"Out taking early lunches, or over at the Cercle Raquette playing tennis. It's really dead. It's like the VC have vanished for good."

"Maybe I'll wander over to MACV and see what's happening there."

Mark smiled. "I think you'll probably get the light-at-the-end-of-the-tunnel speech today. Some colonel will tell you the Vietcong have ceased to be a problem and we'll be pulling out soon. It's very inspiring and very boring."

"There must be something going on," said Morrow.

Mark shook his head. "Couple of mortar attacks reported around the area, but no damage or anyone wounded. I think some Air Force plane was shot at but took no hits."

Morrow checked her messages one last time, but none of them promised anything interesting. She decided she didn't want to call anyone then. "Anything brewing over at the embassy?"

"Nope. Just more talk about the upcoming Lunar Holidays. I think everything is in place for the cease-fire. Then it's really going to be boring around here."

"Yeah," agreed Morrow.

"Say, Robin, since your Green Beret is out in the field, why don't you and I go scare up some lunch."

Morrow looked at the clock that hung over the file cabinets and was surprised to see that the morning was nearly gone. She nodded. "Only if you buy."

"Consider it done."

Morrow stood. "Then by all means, let's go. I'm ready."

FETTERMAN STOOD NEAR THE GATE of Camp A-337 and studied the open ground east of the camp. The rice paddies were filled with muddy, foul water, and clumps of palm, coconut and teak trees protected the mud hootches of the farmers from the tropical sun and the rain-laden monsoons. He stood quietly, his harnesses digging into his shoulders and his sweat dampening and staining his jungle fatigues. On his hip were a first-aid kit and three canteens filled with warm water, as well as the holster that held a Browning M-35 pistol and fourteen rounds in a staggered box magazine. On the harness were grenades, both smoke and fragmentation, and a combat knife taped to the left strap upside down. He could draw it and kill in one smooth, continuous motion if the opportunity presented itself. He hoped it would not.

Timmons stood to the right, near a low bunker covered with the OD green rubberized sandbags that were becoming standard in Vietnam. The jungle climate rotted the old canvas and cloth ones in a matter of weeks, letting the sand spill so that the walls built from them looked like dikes leaking water.

Near him was a rank of Vietnamese soldiers wearing American tiger-striped fatigues, some carrying weapons that had been outdated since World War II. Others had brand-new M-16s that the American Congress and defense industry were so proud of. All the men were waiting for the patrol to begin. They were talking quietly to one another and ignoring the Americans who were also waiting.

Timmons slid to his right and leaned close to Fetterman, speaking in a quiet voice. "You don't have to go out with us," he said. "This is going to be a routine patrol. We'll be back by dusk."

"I know that, Sergeant," responded Fetterman, "but I was ordered to watch your operation, and this is the best way of doing it." Fetterman realized how that must sound and added, "Don't worry about it. I'm not inspecting you. This is just to help you out."

"Right," said Timmons. "And the check is in the mail."

Fetterman had to grin. "Yeah. I know what you mean. Anyway, relax. I'm on your side."

Before Timmons could respond, Gerber and Fulton appeared, approaching from the redoubt. Fulton called out, "You ready to go?"

"Yes, sir," said Timmons.

"Okay. Now remember that I want you back by dusk before I put out the listening posts and the ambush patrols for the night. I don't want you stumbling into them."

Gerber said, "Tony, this really isn't necessary. You don't have to go out on patrol."

"Why is everyone trying to get me to stay in camp?"

Gerber shrugged. "Maybe it's your winning personality and we can't stand the thought of you having fun without us."

"Then you'll have the beer ice-cold on my return?" questioned Fetterman.

Now Fulton leaped into the conversation. "That goes without saying." He hesitated. "Just loop around east and north of the camp. I don't want you getting too far afield. Radio check every thirty minutes on this one."

"Not to worry, Captain," said Timmons. "We have this sucker wired from here to Tuesday."

"See you in a couple of hours," said Fetterman.

"Good luck, Tony," said Gerber.

Fulton pulled Timmons aside and said something to him quietly. Then Timmons turned and waved at the Vietnamese. One of them separated himself from the group and trotted out the gate, slowing as he passed the last strand of the wire.

"Point's out," said Timmons. "Let's move it."

The rest of the Vietnamese moved toward the gate, forming into a single file. Each man kept his weapon slung until he was outside the camp where, once past the wire, he unslung it and jacked a round into the chamber. From that moment he kept his weapon in his hands, a finger on the trigger guard and his thumb on the safety so that he could flip it off in one fluid motion.

After the men left the camp, Gerber looked at Fulton. "Well, Captain, I think I'd like to take a look around."

Fulton smiled. "I've got quite a bit of work that needs to be done. You won't mind if I turn the duty over to Captain Minh, will you?"

Gerber laughed. "You're taking this like it was an inspection. It's not."

"Then you don't mind?"

"Hell, Captain, I'll ask Minh what's wrong here and he'll tell me in no uncertain terms. I worked with him on my first tour. He'll fill me in to a depth I wouldn't be able to obtain if I stayed here for a week. No, I don't mind."

They found Minh working in his office in the Vietnamese section of the camp. At the front end of a hootch, Minh's tiny office contained a dirty plywood floor, a battered desk and a squeaky chair. Overhead, a fan rotated as slowly as the minute hand on a clock. Blowing through the screened upper half of the office, a light breeze rustled the papers on the desk. Outside, to the west, were black storm clouds boiling and threatening rain in the late afternoon.

When they stepped inside, Gerber said, "Thanks, Captain. I'll be fine now."

Fulton nodded and turned, moving across the compound. Minh looked up from the stacks of paper. "What can I do for you?"

"Your counterpart seems to think you'll be able to snow me."

Minh dropped his pen on top of the papers and tented his fingers under his chin. "And do you think it'll work?"

Gerber glanced over his shoulder and spotted a broken-down cloth couch. It might have been green at one time, but the fabric was so dirty and stained that it was hard to tell. He sat down carefully and said, "No reason to snow me. I'm not here to cause any trouble."

"You know we all find that rather hard to accept, old boy, given Saigon's penchant for sticking their noses where they bloody well don't belong."

"And I understand, having experienced the same thing out at our old camp. But you should know me better than that. Even if my orders dictated some kind of inspection, I wouldn't be pulling one. I just want to hear what's going on."

Minh rubbed his face. "Surely."

"How have you been? And why aren't you a major in some soft job in Saigon."

Minh turned and stood up. He walked around the side of his desk and then sat on it so that he was looking down on Gerber. "I'm not a major because my family is too poor to buy the promotion. Not that I mind. If I wanted, I could put together the capital to buy my way out of here."

"Now how in hell—"

Minh held up a hand to stop him. "There are a dozen ways to do it. Your government's throwing money around as if there's no tomorrow. Any inquiry made from your end, initiated by the men in the field, is routinely halted. You don't want to offend your allies, old boy.''

"What?"

"Mack, look around you. All pay and allowances for the strike companies come through my office. Rather than trust your men here, your paymasters are dispatched by the brass from Saigon. They don't know the men here and don't bother inspecting them as they're paid. They sit there and let us handle the duty, believing everything we tell them. It's all based on the approved strength of the strike companies and our reported figures. If I say I have five hundred men in the strike companies, I'm paid for those five hundred men. If thirty of them have deserted, or been killed, or never existed, your paymaster is still ready to pay five hundred men.''

Now Gerber leaned forward. "You mean to tell me—"

"That I could create a phantom company and receive pay for it. If Captain Fulton were to protest, he'd be told to leave the administration of the strike companies to me. It's not his job to interfere with the Vietnamese. After all, you don't want to insult your bloody allies."

"Does this go on?"

"Not here, because I won't allow it, but I know it does at other camps. More than one phantom battalion exists with the officers drawing all that extra money."

"Shit."

"Mack, you don't know the half of it," said Minh. "There are officers drawing equipment for those phantom battalions and then selling it all in Saigon. One pilot told me the only place he can get the Nomex flight gloves he's required to wear is buy them on the black market."

"What a way to fight a war."

"Precisely, old boy." Minh let that soak in and then asked, "Now what did you want to know?"

"How did you end up here?"

Minh shifted so that he was more comfortable. He glanced at the floor. "Good luck, actually. After your men rotated to the States, they brought in another A-team, kept the camp open for six, seven months and then decided we'd all be of better use elsewhere. Closed it down and scattered the men."

"Typical," said Gerber.

"Yes." Minh hopped off the desk. "You want a tour of Plei Soi?"

"Not really. I want to know what's wrong here and what's right. And I want to know when you expect the big push. Seems the intel reports lead to that conclusion."

"I expect the big push to come within the next week and probably much sooner. Too much activity around here for us to expect anything less."

"Good," said Gerber. "You don't know how good that is."

THE PATROL CROSSED THE OPEN FIELDS outside the camp and entered the rice paddies. The point man avoided the dark, calm water and stayed on the dikes. Each man behind him followed by carefully stepping into his footprints.

Fetterman got Timmons's attention and asked, "Shouldn't we be in the paddies?"

Timmons shrugged. "Charlie rarely booby-traps the dikes around here because all he gets are farmers. And if we go walking through the paddies, stepping on the plants as the drill sergeants in the World tell you, then we piss off the farmers.''

''Yeah,'' said Fetterman. He understood what Timmons was saying. If they followed the infantry manual as produced in the World, they'd become a propaganda machine for the enemy—the Americans were out there killing the people's livelihood. And if Charlie wasn't booby-trapping the dikes in the area, then there wasn't any reason to walk across the plants.

They continued on, working their way from one dike to the next, always moving closer to the trees and the hootches, but there was no one in the fields. Overhead was the buzz of helicopters and the occasional roar of jets, but no other sounds. Nothing from the hootches gathered in the trees and nothing from the animals around them.

Fetterman watched the Vietnamese, impressed with their discipline. They kept their weapons ready, their heads moving, searching the fields around them, even though there was no way for Charlie to sneak up on them. They made almost no noise and they didn't talk to one another or smoke. These were among the best-trained Vietnamese he had seen, and he suspected Captain Minh had had a hand in it. He also suspected that these were the best troops in the camp, that they'd been instructed to look good because the brass hat from Saigon would be watching.

As they neared the hootches, they stopped, the patrol scattering slightly. The men slipped from the dikes into the water and crouched there, their weapons held at the ready while Timmons used his binoculars to study the empty hootches.

Fetterman slid into the water, too, and felt it soak his fatigues and pour into his boots. He tried not to inhale the rank odor as he leaned against the dike. Around his head a couple of flies buzzed, and gnats darted in and out like fighters strafing an enemy position.

He watched as the point man moved forward cautiously, using the little cover available, but never screening himself from the men behind him. He crouched low, ran to the side and leaped across the last few feet of the dike, landing on dry ground. He slipped to one knee so that he was shielded from the hootches by the remains of an oxcart, a rotting wagon with a broken wheel that stood fifty meters from a hootch.

Once the point man was in position half the men began to sweep forward. Now they left the dikes, spreading out so that a single enemy gunner couldn't hit them with one well-placed burst, or one grenade couldn't wound them all. The last half of the squad held their positions, covering the men on the move.

Fetterman turned and glimpsed a splash in the water twenty or thirty yards away. It looked like a rifle shot, but he hadn't heard anything. The men moving toward the hootches kept their pace steady, and for a second Fetterman wondered if he'd imagined the splash.

Then there was a ripping burst from one of the hootches that overpowered all sound around it. The bullets stitched the water, creating brownish silver fountains and a fine mist that held a rainbow of colors.

"Incoming," yelled someone. The men dived right and left, landing face first in the foul rice paddy water. A splash of orange erupted on a dike, and the shrapnel from the grenade sliced through the air.

Fetterman flipped off the safety on his M-3 and pointed the weapon at the hootches, but he saw nothing. He scanned the disintegrating line, quickly searching for muzzle-flashes, puffs of burnt gunpowder or movement that would betray the enemy, but there was nothing.

Around him there was firing as the Vietnamese and Timmons opened up with their M-16s. There was a rapid chattering that sounded as if only one or two weapons were firing. The rounds hit the mud walls of the hootches, kicking up gouts of dust and dirt. But there was nothing in return.

Then, in the doorway of one hootch, Fetterman saw a flicker of movement. He turned, aimed and waited until he saw it again. When he did, he pulled his trigger four times, scattering his shots into the darkened door. A moment later a weapon dropped into the sunlight. There was no body, but Fetterman was sure he'd hit someone.

Firing increased then. Not only could he hear the M-16s and M-1s of the strikers, but now there was the rapid fire of AK-47s. From the far right came the hammering of a machine gun, probably a .30-caliber, Soviet-made RPD because of the rate of fire.

Fetterman slipped down until he was nearly prone in the rice paddy, the filthy water lapping at his chin, the stench filling his nostrils. He eased forward, trying not to disturb the water or make a sound, even though the firing of weapons filled the air around him.

There was a snap near his ear, like an angry bee flashing past and he dropped down. The round had passed close to him but wasn't followed by a second. He worked his way to the dike, which ran parallel to the hootches, and stopped. He squinted into the bright sunlight and saw the strikers spread out in front of him.

Timmons was to the right and had slung his weapon. In each hand he held grenades, but he hadn't moved since yanking them from his harness. The shooting seemed to taper, dropping from the nearly constant roar until it was spaced, single shots from the two sides. When that happened, Timmons rocked back, threw the grenade in his right hand and switched the second one over, tossing it, too. He dropped to the side of a dike, one hand pressed down unnecessarily on his helmet.

There were two explosions, both short of the hootches, but as the grenades detonated, Timmons's men were on their feet, running and firing. They spread out, diving for cover behind a lone palm, under the oxcart, near the remnants of a mud fence. As they fell into the cover, they directed their firing into the closest window or doorway. The sporadic popping grew until it sounded like the longest string of firecrackers in the world, set off by three or four fuses.

Fetterman leaped over the dike then and dropped into the muddy water on the other side. He crawled through it rapidly until he was near the dike closest to the hootches. He glanced over the top. There were men running and shooting. One of the strikers rolled under the window of a hootch and chucked a grenade into it. There was a second's delay and a man in black dived out the door as the hootch exploded and the thatch began to smoke heavily.

The man rolled on his stomach and leaped to his feet. He started to run but was hit by rifle fire. His body jerked and he sprawled on the ground, his foot kicking spasmodically as he died.

Fetterman was no longer aware of the rifle fire around him. He ignored the sound of the M-16s and M-1s, concentrating on the enemy weapons. There was an AK to his left, and Fetterman eased along the dike, aware of how bright the sun was and black his shadow was. He didn't want the shadow to give him away, so he hugged the ground, moving slowly and watching the terrain in front of him.

Out of the corner of his eye he saw something rise, and he snapped a look at it. A striker ran left along the mud fence and then dropped by it. He rolled on his back and laid the barrel of his weapon on the top of the fence, firing without being able to aim. When his weapon was empty, he pulled it back, slammed a fresh magazine in and repeated the process.

Fetterman kept moving. He dived behind a bush and rolled into a shallow depression that was filled with mud. He felt the wetness there press against him, but it was no worse than that from the rice paddy. He ignored it as he crawled forward. The sounds of the firing behind him seemed to recede farther into the distance. With one part of his mind, he heard and cataloged the weapons firing, and with another, listened to the sounds close to him: the hammering of his heart, the rasp of the breath in his throat and the buzz of insects near his head. That was the funny thing: he could hear the insects, even as the .30 caliber opened fire again and the bullets snapped through the air above him.

Fetterman hesitated there and then began crawling slowly. He glanced at the hootch in front of him. The walls were pockmarked and there was a hole near the center. The thatched roof was sagging and there was no door.

Moving closer still, he pulled a grenade from his harness, yanked the pin and flipped it away. Then, watching the window, he reared back and threw the grenade into the hootch. As he dropped flat, the air over his head was ripped by machine gun fire. There was an explosion, and smoke and dust boiled out of the window and hole in the mud hootch. Fetterman was on his feet, running. He leaped over a palm log and landed with his back against the side of the hootch. Dirt cascaded around him, making his nose itch, but he refused to sneeze.

He slid to the right, along the wall. As he reached the corner, he stopped. There was a sound from the hootch, and a second later a man appeared, clutching an AK in bloody hands, the bayonet extended. Fetterman grabbed the barrel, jerking the man forward. As the enemy stepped into the light, Fetterman slammed an elbow into his face. There was a crunch of bone and a low moan of pain as the man released his weapon. Fetterman jerked it free and stepped around, bringing his knee up sharply. Without another sound, the man slumped to the ground.

There was an explosion from the other side of the hamlet, and the machine gun stopped firing. Two men shouted and a third screamed as another grenade detonated. And then it was silent. As silent as death.

Fetterman spun and saw that two of the strikers were lying in the dirt while a third worked over them. Timmons was running across an open area. He jumped over a fallen enemy and disappeared into a hootch. A moment later he reappeared, dragging the body of a dead man with him. As soon as he was into the open, he let go of the dead man's shirt.

Fetterman grabbed the unconscious man at his feet and dragged him toward the center of the hamlet. He dropped him near the wounded strikers as Timmons came forward.

"We've got the area secured."

"Where are the farmers?"

Timmons shrugged. "Found a body over on the left. Looks like the man's been dead for two, three days, but given the heat, who can tell? There are a couple of other bodies in the hootches, too. One of them was a woman, dead as long as the farmer in the field. I think that tells us where the farmers are.''

"Any idea of who killed them or why?"

Timmons shrugged. "Farmer was shot, but I can't tell with what. Woman was killed by shrapnel, and then the hootch fell on her. I don't think it was our side, because we'd know about any operations in the area."

Fetterman accepted that and pointed at the unconscious man at his feet. "You notice anything?"

"Such as?"

Fetterman crouched near his prisoner. "This guy's got white side walls. Dressed like a VC, but he's NVA. I've seen this before."

Timmons dropped to one knee and turned the man over. He grabbed one of his hands and inspected it. "This guy's no farmer, that's for sure."

"I suggest we search this hamlet, but I doubt we'll find anything in it now. We ran into the rear guard. I think someone on their side got trigger-happy, or there would have been no one here when we walked in."

Timmons stood. "I'll get my people together and we'll get out of here."

"Let's make a thorough search first. Probably won't be anything to find, but let's not leave any stone unturned just in case."

For a moment Timmons stood, staring at Fetterman, and then said, "Sure."

"Something eating you?" asked Fetterman.

"I know my job."

Fetterman nodded. "I'm sure you do. Sorry, but you have to understand that we old master sergeants are used to telling everyone how to act. I even have suggestions for Captain Gerber, although he's about as smart as I am."

"Okay," said Timmons, smiling. "No sweat."

"By the way," said Fetterman, "did we manage to take the machine gun?"

"We got it," he responded, "but it's in pretty bad shape. Grenade ripped it up."

"Pity."

While Timmons worked his way through the hamlet, checking for wounded enemy soldiers, dropped weapons and documents, Fetterman helped the medic. The wounds were superficial. One striker had taken a round through the triceps, but the bullet had missed the bone, and although painful, it wasn't life threatening. The other man had a piece of shrapnel stuck in his side just above the hip. It bled freely, staining the man's fatigues crimson. The medic pulled it free and then treated the wound.

Timmons and his men found the bodies of twelve dead soldiers. They dragged them into the open and left them lying in the dirt as they continued their inspection. Fetterman moved among them, checking for documents and unit insignia. All but two wore the black pajamas of the VC. The remaining two wore the khaki of the NVA and boots that looked more like tennis shoes. Fetterman searched the pockets and found only a single sheet of paper, which looked like a squad listing. At the top was the unit designation—the 308th Regiment. Fetterman stuffed the paper into his own pocket.

Timmons returned, having completed his sweep of the tiny hamlet. "Found a couple of blood trails and this." He held up a small burlap bag. "Medical kit."

"Let's see it," said Fetterman. He opened it and pawed through the vials and bandages. Many of them were stamped with labels in English, meaning they were stolen from the Americans. One or two had labels that said they were gifts from students in the United States for the People's Army in Vietnam.

"Should we follow the blood trails?"

Fetterman looked at the sun and then at his watch. "Your captain said he wanted you back before dusk. You don't have the time to follow up."

"But we should follow the trails," said Timmons.

"And you have some intelligence that is valuable to the men at the camp," advised Fetterman. "You can report this fight and your observations about the enemy, not to mention the document I found."

"Okay," said Timmons. "I'm not going to argue about a trip back to the camp. I'll get the men organized."

"Be sure we get all the weapons." He held up a hand. "Yes, even the damaged machine gun. Charlie might strip it and use the parts and metal to repair other machine guns. We leave him nothing."

Timmons asked, "You think this fight is significant?"

Fetterman watched as the men retreated slowly, leaving their advance positions and drawing back into a defensive circle around the wounded men. He approved of the caution shown by the strikers.

To Timmons he said, "The fact they were here, this close to your camp, is significant. I'll need to check the intel reports to see if the unit designation means anything, but yes, I think we have some significant intel here."

The men were ready then, having picked up everything of use to the enemy. Two men had even collected the brass expended during the firefight, making sure the VC wouldn't be able to collect it later. With that, Timmons sent out his point man, and they began the trek back across the rice paddies to Camp A-337.

5

SPECIAL FORCES HEADQUARTERS, NHA TRANG

Sergeant Andy Santini sat behind his battered gray desk and faced the small electric fan that was trying to stir the thick air into a breeze. He sat with his polished but not spit-shined boots propped on the corner of his desk, his pressed but not starched jungle fatigue jacket unbuttoned so that his sweat-soaked OD green T-shirt was visible. He held a file folder in his hand so that he looked busy. Periodically he wiped the sweat from his face with his sleeve, leaving a ragged wet stain there.

Santini was a small man who looked like Fetterman from a distance. Although he was clean-shaven, he had thick eyebrows over brown eyes and a nearly permanent five o'clock shadow. He had a thin face with a pointed chin and nose and a dark complexion that was probably the result of heredity rather than the hot tropical sun.

He jerked upright when a voice from the inner office shouted, "Santini!"

The sergeant dropped his feet to the floor and leaped across the dirty plywood. He centered himself in the doorway to Major Frank Madden's office. "Yes, sir?"

The walls of the inner office were made of thin plywood and painted a sickening light green. A bamboo mat sat on the plywood floor in front of another beat-up desk. There were a couple of metal folding chairs and a ripped, stained settee along one wall. On another wall hung the Special Forces crest with the legend *De Oppresso Liber*.

"You seen this?" asked the man behind the desk. He was a thin man with a receding hairline. He had a thick black mustache in contrast to his thinning, graying hair. Sweat stained the underarms of his fatigues.

Santini moved across the floor carefully. Major Madden had been asked to extend his tour when Gerber and Fetterman had gotten themselves in hot water in the Hobo Woods. Madden was an unhappy man, figuring he should have been back in the World chasing women in incredibly short skirts instead of sitting in Nha Trang sweating with a sour stomach. He blamed it all on Gerber and Fetterman.

"If those two would stay out of trouble for a couple of days, I might be able to get the fuck out of here," said Madden. "Just a couple of days."

Santini took the paper. It was a letter from a colonel in Saigon saying that Gerber and Fetterman were now out looking over a Special Forces camp—a fact-finding tour to determine the disposition of the camp at Plei Soi.

"They keep sticking it to me," said Madden. "I want you to hotfoot it over to S-2 and see what's cooking in that area. Couple it with what we know is going down in the north and I'll bet my DEROS those two clowns are in the thick of it again. Somehow they always end up in the middle of it, and I end up getting fucked again."

"And if they are, sir?" asked Santini, not sure that anything they did would matter.

"Then I want some of our people ready to haul ass to get them out of trouble. You set up something here, a reaction team to coordinate with me and then you go to Moc Hoa and see about arranging for the Mike Force there to be used if Plei Soi gets hit and needs our help. That's our contingency plan if things degenerate rapidly."

"Aren't you jumping the gun, sir?"

Madden sat up straighter and glared at Santini. "You trying to irritate me, Sergeant? 'Cause if you're not, you're coming real close. Did it occur to you I might have looked over the intel reports from the area and have an idea of what's going down near there? Did it occur to you I might know a little more than those clowns in Saigon?"

"Yes, sir."

"So now I want you to run over there and check with the intel section and see if anything new has been added. Get yourself a good briefing on the enemy situation in the Plei Soi area. Then you come and tell me. Can you handle that?"

"Yes, sir. Sorry, sir." Santini turned and then faced the major again. "You want me to take Kit?"

"Now why in hell would you ask that?"

"Only that as a former VC she might have an idea what they're doing, meaning the Vietcong, and she's familiar with the AO."

Madden shook his head. "That's what you say every time. First she's familiar with the Hobo Woods, which is, I might point out, forty or fifty miles away from Camp A-337. Now you tell me she's familiar with that area."

Santini shrugged. "She got around when she was with the enemy, sir."

"Well, Sergeant Got Around, I want you over in S-2, and if you find something where her talents are required, then we might have Miss Emilie assigned to you and the Mike Force. But it's going to take a special circumstance."

"Yes, sir." Santini returned to his own office, slid the file folder he had been reading into his desk and then switched off his fan. With his office and desk cleared, he walked out the front, took the jeep assigned to Major Madden and drove toward the recon school. He turned off and parked in front of a large bunker surrounded by barbed wire and guarded by armed MPs. This was the intelligence command.

At the gate he was stopped by an MP who checked his ID, then consulted an access roster to make sure Santini was cleared. Once that was established, Santini was allowed to enter so he could sign in, but he was cautioned against carrying anything out of the bunker or making notes. Finally he was given a badge to clip on to his jungle fatigue jacket.

Santini entered the bunker and found it much cooler than outside. He descended a short flight of filthy wooden stairs and walked down a narrow hallway. The walls were made of thick wooden planks that bled sap and smelled dirty. The floor was littered with crushed cigarettes and small piles of dirt, the latter having seeped from the dozen layers of sandbags that made up most of the bunker's structure. There were doors cut into the wall, but all of them were closed, some of them with combination locks.

Turning into a dimly lit corridor that reeked of dust and sweat, he came to a door and knocked on it. There was a moment's hesitation, then a small window in the center of the door opened and a face peered out at him.

"Sergeant Santini to see Captain Branert."

The window closed and the door opened. Santini stepped into the brightly lighted interior where two NCOs sat working behind tables. A corporal stood in a corner trying to look busy. Maps hung on all the walls, many of them with big red secret stamps on them. Some of the maps were illuminated with small lights, which made them look like high-priced paintings in a gallery. American units were marked in bright blue and enemy forces were marked in red. Due to all the red encircling it, the area around Nui Ba Den in Tay Ninh Province looked as if it had been cut and had hemorrhaged.

Santini was looking at the map, trying to figure out all the enemy unit designations, both Vietcong and NVA, when Branert entered. He was a tall thin man with a mass of brown hair that was longer than regulations said it should be and looked as if it had never been combed. His skin was pasty white, indicating he rarely left his bunker and was never in the field. His fatigues were dirty and wrinkled, and Santini wondered how often Branert went out. He knew there were some men who spent their tours in bunkers on the larger American bases hiding from the rockets and mortars.

"Sir," said Santini, "Major Madden over at SFHQ wanted me to see the latest intel updates on the enemy in the Tay Ninh area."

"Again?" said Branert, running a hand through his hair. "Things look the same this afternoon as they did this morning." He shook his head as if he couldn't believe the request. "Hold on and I'll see what we have."

Santini moved closer to one of the sergeants. "He ever go outside?"

"Hear he went to a show once. Some round-eyed band from Australia was playing at the club and he went to see it, but on the way back somebody on the bunker line fired a weapon and the captain vowed not to see the sun until DEROS. He eats down here, and his friends come down here to visit him. Had a shower installed in the rear, and our corporal here gets to carry water to it when the barrel feeding it runs dry. It's all quite unbelievable.''

"Christ."

"You know it."

Branert returned, holding a bunch of papers with a red cover sheet on them. He removed the top sheet and stepped to the map, checking the enemy units with the information in the file he carried.

"Okay, Sergeant, here's the poop. We have indications of four major regiments in northern Tay Ninh Province. There are elements of the Twelfth NVA Division north of there and several unidentified maneuver battalions along with miscellaneous companies and platoons. Many of them have only recently been identified and are therefore considered new to the region, though they might have been there for a month or more.''

"What's the enemy troop strength in this area?" asked Santini, pointing to the map near Camp A-337.

"Round numbers and within fifty miles, I'd say, three, four thousand."

"Christ!"

"That's up from maybe eight hundred."

Santini took a step back. "You don't think that's significant? You don't think that's something we should have given to the men in the field out there?"

"Hell, man, it's nothing to get your bowels in an uproar over. Charlie is always moving through that area. Numbers will peak and then drop off dramatically until it's back to normal. There's nothing to report to the local commander. Besides, his own patrols should be supplying him with this information. I shouldn't have to get it for him.''

''The major know this?''

Branert smiled, showing yellow teeth. His breath wrapped around Santini like a fog. ''Gave it to him this morning. Then it became his responsibility to make sure the proper briefs were forwarded. I've done my job.''

Santini nodded. ''That explains his bad mood.''

IT WAS NEARLY DUSK when Fetterman and the patrol reached the outer wire of the camp. When they reached the flimsy gate, two of the Vietnamese from inside the camp ran out to help. Timmons directed them to take the wounded men over to the dispensary so that the senior medic could treat them.

Once inside the compound, Fetterman pushed the prisoner to the front of the patrol. When three more strikers left the camp, Fetterman turned the prisoner over to them, telling them, ''See that the intel NCO is told that we've taken this man. He'll want to talk to him.'' Fetterman caught the look of unrestrained hatred on the face of one of the strikers and said, ''Remember, a dead man can tell us nothing, but a living prisoner can keep some of our people alive, too.'' As they escorted the enemy soldier into the camp, Fetterman was sure he had convinced them of the philosophy.

Timmons turned toward the remainder of the men and shouted, ''Weapons check in twenty minutes. Then we'll find some chow. Questions?''

When no one spoke, the patrol split up. Timmons led Fetterman into the redoubt. ''I have to report to Captain Fulton,'' he said.

"Right," agreed Fetterman. "And I need to talk with Captain Gerber. You'd better make sure your intel specialist is over there, too, so that he can look over the documents. That is, after he looks in on the prisoner."

"Sergeant Clement doesn't read Vietnamese all that well," said Timmons.

Fetterman grinned. "Then why in hell is he the intel specialist out here?"

"Best man we could get."

"Well, I can read it after a fashion, and given what we've seen today, I think it's a fairly important document. Maybe the two of us can puzzle it out if we put our heads together."

Fetterman found Gerber and Fulton together in the team house, eating sandwiches and drinking coffee, waiting for him to return from the patrol. He dropped his webgear on the floor and pushed it out of the way with his foot. He then sat down, took Gerber's coffee and drained the cup.

"You want the rest of my sandwich, too, Master Sergeant?" asked Gerber.

"No, sir. Just the coffee for now. Thought you and I should have a little chat about what I saw."

Gerber shot a glance at Fulton. "If you'll excuse me for a few minutes."

"No problem," said Fulton.

Gerber stood, and Fulton moved toward the door. Fetterman watched as Timmons appeared suddenly, having shed his pack. He stopped near the refrigerator and got a beer. Timmons grinned at him and tossed it. Fetterman snagged it out of the air with a quick snap of his wrist.

"Thought you could use a cold one," said Timmons as he pulled a second can out for himself.

"Thanks."

Once they were outside, into the darkening of the humid night, Gerber asked, "Well?"

"I think they're in for some real trouble in the very near future."

"Meaning?"

Fetterman popped the top on the can and dropped the ring into the open can. "Meaning that we ran into a small unit that sacrificed itself to pin us down for fifteen or twenty minutes. I mean, given the circumstances, I would have expected the enemy to flee the moment we returned fire in a coordinated fashion. Instead they hung on and let us kill most of them."

Gerber nodded. "So you think you ran into a rear guard that let the larger unit get away, let it get out of sight before you ran into it?"

"Yes, sir. I think they didn't take us because it would have raised too big a stink. I think they let us at those guys so we'd think we'd got them all. I think it means the big push is coming tonight or tomorrow at the latest. Otherwise they'd have taken us."

"That's pretty thin reasoning, Tony. You might have run into the whole unit and killed them all."

"I thought of that, Captain," said Fetterman. He took a drink from his beer and stared into the night. "But there is this paper." He touched his pocket. "I thought it was a squad pay roster, but now I'm not so sure. I wish I could read Vietnamese better, but from what I could pick up, it's the pay for a headquarters company staff attached to the People of Mo Hue Regiment, and they haven't been identified as being in this area."

"Shit," said Gerber. "Another regiment, added to all the others that are around."

"Exactly, Captain. That's why I think we ran into a rear guard."

Gerber turned his attention to the night sky. The clouds he'd seen boiling over Cambodia were moving in. The ceiling was dropping so that it was only a couple of hundred feet above the ground. The bad weather would bring rain and wind and keep the Air Force at bay. It would also keep the helicopters away, because they would have to come in low, under the clouds where they could be picked off like so many clay pigeons.

"Okay, Tony, I think you may be right. If the weather gets much worse, they'll hit us tonight because it'll be the best opportunity for it to happen."

Almost as if to prove the point, he heard the distant pop of a mortar tube firing. Instead of dropping to the ground, Gerber spun, scanning the horizon to the northeast of the camp where he thought the sound had come from. There was a second pop, but he didn't see the flash.

A moment later there was a crash in the wire a hundred yards away. The burst of light, like a Fourth of July display, illuminated the wire around it and then was lost in the cascade of dirt.

Fetterman fell to one knee and looked up at Gerber. "Incoming."

"I know that." He waited, then saw the second detonation to the west of the first. "They're not coming toward us."

"Yes, sir" was Fetterman's response.

There was a whoosh overhead and a loud, flat bang that echoed throughout the camp. Gerber dropped, then looked at the haze of dust and smoke created by the detonation of the rocket. He turned and crawled to a sandbagged bunker on the perimeter. In the distance he saw a flash.

"There. Got it." He leaped to his feet and ran toward the command post at the base of the fire control tower. As he reached it, he heard the roar of the rocket's engine and dived to the ground with his hands over his ears.

The explosion was closer this time. Dirt and debris rained down on his back. Gerber was up again, running through the choking cloud of cordite and dust. He jumped for the door of the command bunker and hit the sandbagged wall, causing loose dirt to cascade around him. Before descending, he glanced back. Fetterman was running toward the redoubt. Around them were the pops of mortar tubes as the enemy got into the rhythm of firing. Small explosions decorated the darkening compound. A fire raged in one of the Vietnamese hootches as men ran around it, trying to put it out.

Gerber scrambled down the stairs and landed on the thick planks of the bunker floor. He saw two men hunched in the corner, as if hiding. A Special Forces sergeant stood with a field phone receiver in one hand and a PRC-25 handset in the other. He was speaking rapidly into the radio.

"Anyone in the FCT?"

"Sergeant Jones is up there," answered the sergeant, his face grim.

Gerber didn't recognize him. "Have they spotted the enemy weapons?"

"Got a tube to the north."

"Okay," said Gerber wiping a hand over his face. He took a deep breath to calm himself and ordered, "Instruct your mortar pits to swing around to 145 degrees with a range of about six hundred meters. Rocket team is there. I spotted the flash on that last volley.''

The sergeant nodded and gave the order. Then he looked at Gerber. ''Won't they be gone now? Rocket teams can get out quickly once they've launched.''

''Let's hope they're hanging around to fire another volley at us.''

With that, he turned and ran up the stairs. For a moment he crouched in the entrance, ready to dive back. There was firing on the perimeter now, but Gerber was sure it was the strikers shooting at shadows. Charlie wouldn't begin his assault until it was darker and he had softened the camp some more. He would wait until most of the buildings were on fire so that many of the men would be distracted fighting the fires, then the enemy gunners would concentrate on destroying the bunkers.

There was another loud bang as a rocket hit the compound. Dirt and shrapnel pelted the sandbags of the command bunker. Gerber smelled the burnt powder again. An acrid stink that reminded him of the fireworks displays of his youth. A festive odor that was now deadly.

Without a conscious thought, he pulled his pistol from his holster. He had left his rifle in the team house where Fulton and Timmons could watch it. He hadn't expected the enemy to launch their attack so early in the evening. But then he hadn't expected the weather to deteriorate quite as rapidly, either.

There seemed to be a lull in the mortars. He jumped clear of the bunker and ran to the redoubt. He skidded to a halt and then, crouching by the dirt-and-sandbag wall, he looked east toward the bunker line. The firing there had increased. Small arms rattled, and the big .50-caliber machine gun chugged, kicking softball-sized tracers into the night. Gerber could see them float across the rice paddies east of the camp, blazing a trail of bright, glowing red. When they hit something solid, they bounced high, tumbling through the air and looking almost harmless.

There was a shout behind him and he turned. Fulton was running toward him, a dark, crouched shape holding two rifles. When he was close, he tossed one to Gerber.

"Thought you'd like this," he called out.

Gerber caught it in his left hand and then jacked a round into the chamber. He holstered his pistol, feeling a little better now that he had a rifle. "Yeah, thanks. What about extra ammo for it?"

"We've ammo stashed all over the compound in case Charlie gets inside the wire and we're cut off from the main ammo bunkers."

"Doesn't that provide the enemy with re-arm?"

"If they're inside the wire, there's not a lot we can do that's going to help them anymore, but the stashed ammo might save us."

"Right. What's the plan now?"

Fulton ducked down and then stood to peek over the top of the wall. He dropped again, a hand on his helmet. "Ride this out. I'm going to the FCT and try to spot some of their tubes. If we do, we might be able to get one of the fire support bases to drop some artillery on them."

"What about your own tubes?"

"I'd like to use the 81s for illumination if we get to that and use the 60s as antipersonnel, if they make a run on the camp. Let the cannon-cockers at the fire support bases have some of the fun."

Before Gerber could respond, there was a wild burst of firing from the northeast side of the camp. Dozens of weapons, machine guns and grenades went off suddenly, but it was all outgoing.

"What the fuck now?" asked Fulton.

"Those are all ours," said Gerber. "I don't hear an AK in the bunch."

"I better go check it out."

"Where would you like Sergeant Fetterman and me?" asked Gerber.

Fulton looked at Gerber. "You been through this before, haven't you?"

Gerber suddenly remembered the assault on his camp when a reinforced regiment had hit them before they had gotten the camp built. Fighting had degenerated into hand-to-hand with the VC inside the wire.

"Yeah. Once or twice."

Fulton wiped his lips with the back of his hand. "Look, get over to the command bunker and wait there. That might be the best thing for now."

"I won't be of much help hidden inside. I need to be out where I can see things."

Suddenly both men dropped flat on the ground, neither of them speaking. Again Gerber put his hands over his ears and opened his mouth. Twenty feet away there was a crash as a mortar round penetrated the tin roof of a hootch and exploded inside. Fire blossomed and the smoke boiled out.

"Shit," said Fulton.

"Anyone in there?"

Fulton put a restraining hand on Gerber's sleeve. "No. Everyone's in the bunkers or on the line."

"Fire-fighting equipment."

"Can't worry about it now," said Fulton. "We'll have to let it burn."

"Look, if you see Fetterman, send him over to me, then find us a place on the line. We'll help out."

Fulton was on his feet again. "Right. I'll see what the dummies were shooting at and then I'll be back."

Fulton glanced around rapidly and then took off at a dead run. He disappeared into the gloom as another volley of mortar rounds landed outside the redoubt.

Gerber turned and jogged around the outside of the redoubt, staying close to the wall. He stopped and listened to the shooting around him, surprised he could hear the weapons. Usually he wasn't aware of the heavy firing. He listened instead for the sound of enemy weapons, now that he could hear the strikers firing from the bunker line. A hundred of them hammered away at the inky blackness around him. Charlie had picked the perfect night: low-hanging clouds blotted out the stars and moon and kept the Air Force on the ground. Just perfect.

He hesitated, breathing rapidly, realizing it was from the excitement and not from running. He felt the sweat drip down his face and along his sides. Through the darkness he could see the opening of the command bunker—a black space like the yawning mouth of a shark. The last thing he wanted to do was get pinned down in a bunker. It was too easy for the enemy to hold you there with a single intelligent sniper.

He ran to it and dropped to the ground next to the entrance. He lay there, turned so that he could see the black slash that was the bunker line. It was all that separated him from the enemy regiment that had to be gathering out there.

And then the mortars and rockets began falling again. Dozens of them slammed into the camp. The explosions flashed all around him, and the whirling of the shrapnel seemed to drown out the sounds of the firing by the strikers.

Gerber slipped closer to the wall of sandbags but didn't duck inside the bunker. He wanted to be out where he could watch the open fields around the camp and search for signs that the enemy was massing for the assault. He got to one knee, his back against the sandbags. He listened to the sounds of the mortars falling around him and to the crackle of the flames as the wooden structures caught fire.

Fetterman loomed out of the darkness and dropped to the ground near him. "What do you think, Captain?"

"Seems like they'll be swarming over us in a couple of minutes." To the right, near the west wall, there were fires burning. A dozen of them lit up the night sky as the hootches burned.

Then they heard a crash, and lightning flashed. In the strobe of the lightning, Gerber saw the outlines of everything around him. The air began to buzz and it started to rain, not a drizzle or a shower but a downpour that wrapped everything in an impenetrable gray mist. Even the flames of the burning hootches were lost in it.

"That's all we need!" yelled Fetterman over the noise of the rain.

Gerber got to his feet and stepped into the sheltering entrance of the command bunker. He shouted, "I'd better get on the horn and see what I can do to get us some help. We're going to need it."

Just as Gerber finished speaking, Charlie renewed his attack, and the mortar rounds started coming down faster than the rain.

6

AIR FORCE COMPLEX AT
NHA TRANG

Santini stood outside the terminal in the humid night air, wishing they could pick up a breeze from the sea. The floodlights from the tower created a pool of light near him. There were four men standing close to him, each wearing jungle fatigues that had been faded by the tropical sun and repeated washings in the chemical laundries operated by the Army.

An Air Force C-130 landed, taxied and then stopped near the terminal. The pilot never shut down the engines or turned off the landing lights. An Air Force sergeant ran from the terminal building, faced the men waiting and shouted over the roaring engines.

"Flight to Saigon is here. If you've processed through operations and been manifested, you can board. If you haven't, please see me."

Santini picked up his gear and weapon and boarded the plane. The interior was no quieter than it had been on the ramp. He stumbled over a couple of people. The troop seats were jammed together along the fuselage, with a double row set back-to-back down the center of the aircraft so that there was almost no legroom. Each of the men had his equipment piled at his feet or held in his lap.

Santini worked his way to the rear of the plane, trying not to fall on anyone. He found an empty seat, dropped his gear on the deck and sat down. He twisted right and left until he found both pieces of the seat belt. Unlike those on commercial aircraft, this was a large thing with a lever and a hook that fit into a metal loop backed by leather. Once he got that done, the loadmaster came toward him and held out a box that contained throwaway earplugs.

When everyone was seated, the loadmaster shut the door and then moved to the rear of the aircraft. The lights dimmed and the noise of the engines increased. The plane vibrated as it began to taxi. Santini glanced at the men who sat across from him. They were dressed in sweat-soaked jungle fatigues. The sweat glistened on their faces. None of them spoke, and a couple of them tried to sleep.

The roar from the engines grew as they rushed down the runway. The C-130 struggled into the air, and the servos made a hideous whine as the landing gear was retracted. Santini was certain the plane was about to crash. He tried not to look scared. He held his breath, but then the servos quieted and the vibrations ceased. One of the men across from him lit a cigarette, and the loadmaster climbed up on the rear ramp and stretched out.

Santini moved his arm, dug his elbow into the side of the man next to him and yelled, "Sorry!" He checked the time and then leaned back, trying to relax. It would be a while before he got to Saigon, and once there he would still have to arrange a flight out to Moc Hoa, which wouldn't be easy at night. He wished he had managed to talk Madden into letting Kit come along, but that hadn't worked out. She was still in Nha Trang.

IT HAD BEEN TEN MINUTES since the last mortar round had fallen. Gerber crouched in the door of the command bunker and watched the fires burn. He looked to the left, through the rain that had slowed since the first cloudburst, and saw that a nearby hootch was still burning. In the flickering light he could see that the one next to it was little more than a pile of smoking rubble.

Fetterman stepped close. "I make it another twelve, fifteen minutes before they start the next mortar attack."

"Just time enough for them to survey the damage and try to target the areas that haven't been hit."

"Where's Fulton?"

"I don't know. We could go and look for him, or we could just take over the west wall. I'll bet the main attack comes from there."

Fetterman shook his head, then realized Gerber wouldn't be able to see the gesture in the dark. "No, sir. From the north. The jungle there provides a perfect staging area, and it's closer to the wire than the Cambodian border."

"Okay, Tony, I'll buy that. But they're going to feint against the other walls to pin us down."

"All I'm saying, Captain, is that we should get to the north wall and wait. That's where it's going to happen."

Gerber turned and leaned against the rough, rubberized sandbags. He wiped his forehead with the damp sleeve of his jungle fatigues. "I'll find Fulton and tell him we'll be on the north wall, waiting for the attack there."

"While you're doing that I'll swing by the ammo bunker and see if there's anything in there we can take with us."

Gerber looked at his watch, peeling the camouflage strap back so that he could see the time. He was surprised when he saw that it wasn't quite nine o'clock. So much had happened already that it seemed more like midnight.

"I'll see you in five minutes," he told Fetterman. Then he leaped from hiding and ran around the edge of the redoubt. He entered it and stopped. Even in the rain the fires still burned. Debris, bits of wood, ripped sandbags, tin from the roofs, plywood and equipment were scattered all over the interior. Some of it smoked, the flames extinguished by the rain. Smoke drifted from the fires as the rain tried to drown them.

Four men stood close to what had been the team house. They were using entrenching tools to throw dirt at the flames but were having no luck suppressing them. The rain, however, was beating down the fire for them.

Jones was on his knees, chopping at the muddy dirt. Gerber ran to him. "How are things here?"

"Not good. We've lost most everything. The ancillary radios are gone and the tunnel that connected the command post with the team house has collapsed."

"Casualties?"

Jones shook his head. He turned and watched as the last standing wall collapsed, fanning the fire outward. A column of glowing embers climbed skyward in a burst of bright sparks, but it died quickly. "That's it then."

"Casualties?" repeated Gerber.

"Yes," said Jones. "Minor so far. Couple of our guys got clipped by shrapnel. I think the Viets had one or two killed, but their medics are working on it. Helping the wounded, that is.''

"Sergeant," said Gerber, "I think we can expect a ground assault soon. I think you'd better get your people to their posts and stand by."

Jones looked up into the rain. "Charlie would come in this. He loves it."

"And it keeps our planes on the ground. This one is going to be our strikers against his infantry. We'll see how good you guys did training them."

"You'll find them up to the task."

"Right. Do you know where Captain Minh is?"

"If he's not in the fire control tower, I imagine he'll be on the south wall."

"Thanks," said Gerber. He decided he was going to check out the south wall first because it would give him a chance to assess the damage there. He ran out of the redoubt and turned south. The ground around him was littered with damaged and broken equipment and the remains of the hootches. There were broken two-by-fours, sections of screen, chunks of plywood, and tin from the roofs lying all over the ground. He passed one hootch that had taken a rocket through the roof. The tin was gone, blown into shrapnel, but all four walls still stood. The windows, the screening and the doors had all been blown out. Paper soaked by the rain was scattered around the hootch, looking like freshly fallen snow.

Gerber avoided the mess and came up on the south wall. He moved to the center where the command bunker stood. Dropping into it, he asked, "Captain Minh?"

"Guessed right, old boy."

Gerber moved forward so that he was near the firing port. He looked out but could see little in the rain. He thought he could see the vibrations of some of the beer cans hung in the wire as they reflected the firelight.

"How do things look here?"

"Right now, not bad. We've a full load of ammo and all the weapons are in working order."

Gerber sat down on an ammo crate and wiped the rainwater from his face. "I think this is the big push tonight."

"I would agree. Charlie won't get any better weather. He might have to rush, but I think he'll hit us."

"Tony said he thought the main attack would come on the north." Gerber was making a statement.

"I agree. Better cover. But he'll want to hit all four sides to pin us down and keep us from shifting the majority of our strength to one side to repel his assault."

"Yeah, well, I was thinking we could reinforce the north wall and have a surprise for him there. Keep small forces on the other walls in case he gets real cute. To make it work, though, we'd need good communication between all four walls."

"I'll tell you what, old boy. I'll leave my exec in command here and go find Captain Fulton. We'll see what we can arrange."

"Let's do it."

Gerber stepped to the entrance and looked up at the rain. As he edged out, he heard a distant pop. He dropped to one knee and felt the water soak through, not that it mattered. Glancing over his shoulder, he said, "Incoming."

The round fell short, tearing up a small section of wire fifty or sixty feet away. A second mortar dropped close to it and then the rounds began walking off to the west.

"They're targeting the wire. They'll be coming soon," said Minh.

"I'm going to the north wall," Gerber yelled.

"I'm right behind you," said Minh.

Without waiting to see where the Vietnamese officer was, Gerber sprinted into the dark. He avoided the last of the burning hootches, the fires nearly all out now, helped by the rain.

He leaped over a fifty-five-gallon drum lying on its side, ran past the entrance to the redoubt, then passed the command bunker. He stopped short of the bunker line when he heard a series of pops in the distance. He crouched, waiting and listening, and when the mortars fell short he ran forward. He stopped at the rear of the main bunker and stood up straight. Holding his hands against his eyes to shield them from the rain, he surveyed the wire in front of him.

Because of the light rain and mist, he couldn't see very far beyond the first or second strand of wire. The strobelike flashes of the mortar detonations proved that Charlie wasn't advancing on them yet; he wouldn't risk dropping the rounds on his own men, but it wouldn't be long. Once he had taken out a few huge chunks of the wire, the sappers would move forward with their satchel charges, determined to blow paths through the defenses. If the enemy could get close enough, he'd blow up several of the bunkers to create a gap in the line.

From the corner came a burst of outgoing fire. Red tracers danced into the night, disappearing into the dark and rain. The chattering was from a .30-caliber machine gun, and Gerber could see the muzzle-flashes marking its position. Before he could move, there were two explosions near the bunker—mortars directed at the machine gun. But even though it fell silent, Gerber could see that the bunker hadn't been hit.

Fetterman approached from the rear loaded with M-16 ammo. He had slung his M-3 grease gun over one shoulder and had an M-16 over the other. "Found a couple of LAWs, an M-79 that no one was using and all the ammo I could carry for the M-16s."

"I didn't talk to Fulton."

"Doesn't matter, Captain. It's his camp and he knows what has to be done."

"Told Minh," said Gerber. "He thinks you're right. We're going to try to reinforce the north wall."

There was a series of crashes behind them—explosions from mortar rounds as Charlie tried to destroy the fire control tower.

Gerber laughed. "Dumb fuck doesn't realize that mortars are worthless in mud. It absorbs the impact and the shrapnel."

"Yeah, but he's got a lot of the rounds so he probably doesn't care. Besides, tomorrow when he takes this camp, he'll have all the ammo he wants."

Gerber shot a glance at Fetterman. "You don't suppose Fulton mined the ammo bunkers, arms locker and heavy weapons the way we used to, do you?"

"I would think, Captain, that if Fulton didn't think of it himself his team sergeant would have done it. That's saved more than one camp."

Again Gerber wiped the rain from his face. He shook his hand. "Let's get ready for them. We need to establish lima-lima contact with the command post and the fire control tower."

"Yes, sir," said Fetterman. He disappeared into the bunker, taking enough weapons, ammo and equipment with him for an entire squad.

MADDEN STAYED IN THE RADIO ROOM, listening to the traffic being relayed from all over South Vietnam. The HF radios, as well as the UHF and the FM, allowed SFHQ in Nha Trang to remain in contact with the A-Detachments that were stationed throughout Southeast Asia. Madden was interested in what was happening at Plei Soi, so he was ignoring most of the traffic.

When he heard that the mortar attacks had started at Camp A-337, he waited to be sure that they were the beginning of the assault. As the rounds continued to fall and more of the buildings in the camp were destroyed, Madden recognized it as the pattern the enemy had used before—a sustained rocket and mortar attack that wiped out the structures, followed by a ground assault to kill the defenders. It usually began after midnight, but the weather was so bad that Charlie was making use of it.

Convinced it was the real thing, he moved deeper into the radio room and touched the shoulder of the sergeant working there. He was a large man, dressed in an OD T-shirt, fatigue pants and shower shoes.

"Sergeant," said Madden, "I need to speak with the commanding officer of either the Crusaders in Tay Ninh or the Hornets at Cu Chi." He thought for a minute, then added, "And the Little Bears."

"Yes, sir." The sergeant sat down and slid his chair along the floor until he came to the SOI. He opened it and flipped through it until he found the radio frequencies used by the units that Madden had designated.

"The Crusaders are the 187th Assault Helicopter Company," he said.

"That's right."

"Crusader Operations, this is Werewolf Six. I say again. Crusader Operations, this is Werewolf Six."

There was a moment of silence, then a faint response. "Werewolf Six, this is Crusader Operations. Go."

The sergeant turned and handed the microphone to Madden. "It's all yours, sir."

"Crusader Operations, is your Six or your Three available?"

"That's a negative. '

"Are they nearby?"

"That's a roger. I've dispatched a runner to locate one or the other."

"Roger that," said Madden. "Say weather at your location."

"Weather is deteriorating rapidly. We have low cloud cover in rain. Visibility is down to a quarter mile and winds are strong and gusting."

Madden looked at the sergeant, then at the wall across the plywood floor from him. Lost in the shadows was a situation map that hadn't been updated for several hours.

Then, over the radio, he heard, "Werewolf Six, this is Crusader Six."

"Roger, Six. We have a situation developing that may require airlift support in the very near future."

There was a hesitation and then, "Be advised that weather conditions are limiting the scope of our operations for the next ten to twelve hours."

Madden glanced at the clock and realized the man was telling him that the Crusaders were grounded until daylight. "This situation may go critical on us. Airlift would be essential."

"Understood, but with the weather there's no way we could put a flight into anywhere around here if it's hot. We'd lose the helicopters."

"We need to have you on standby," said Madden.

"That's no problem. We can have the crews standing by the helicopters so that we can take off as soon as the weather breaks for us."

"Could you move the helicopters to Moc Hoa?"

Again there was a hesitation. "That's negative."

Madden frowned at the sergeant. "Roger. Please have your people standby. We may need the help." He was about to sign off when a thought struck him. "Can we have a ship for Medevac?"

"Is the need immediate?"

"Negative. It's a contingency."

"Roger. I'll have a crew standing by for that. Single ship should be able to handle it."

"Roger that. Thanks."

Madden had similar results with the Hornets and the Little Bears. Each aviation unit commander wanted to help, but the rain and low cloud cover made it impossible. They would have to come in so low that the enemy would be able to pick them off easily. In the rain and darkness it would be impossible to maintain unit integrity. Each said they would supply a single ship for Medevac and resupply, and when the weather broke, they could be off in a matter of minutes.

Madden gave the microphone back to the sergeant and slumped against the counter. He shook his head. "I hope those men don't need help tonight, because I don't know how we're going to get it out to them."

As soon as the C-130 bounced to the ground and rolled to a halt, Santini was on his feet. He pushed past a number of men who stared at him but said nothing. He got to the front as the loadmaster opened the hatch. In a second he was on the tarmac, the roaring of the plane's engines filling the night. Looking to the right, Santini ran toward the lights of the operations building.

Inside he used a field phone to call for a jeep, using Major Madden's name. That done, he retreated outside and paced up and down in front of the building, waiting for the jeep. Overhead the clouds were moving in, and there was the smell of rain in the air. He wished he smoked so that he'd have something to do, something that would take his mind off the weather and give him some way to mark the passing of time. Somewhere he had read that it took seven minutes to smoke a cigarette.

And then, before he could get worried, a jeep driven by a master sergeant pulled up and the driver asked, "You seen a Major Madden?"

Santini plucked his gear from the ground and tossed it into the back. "Major Madden's not here. He called for me."

"Sure he did, Sergeant."

"Major Madden's my boss. He arranged transport to Hotel Three for me."

The sergeant, a fat dumpy-looking man with dark hair who wore a flak jacket just in case, shook his head and muttered, "Just what the fuck I wanted to do—drive some sorry-ass sergeant around."

"Yeah," said Santini. "Maybe you'd like me to drive you around and then you can fly out to Moc Hoa for me."

"Smart-ass." The sergeant jammed the jeep into gear with a grinding noise.

They roared off the airfield. The sergeant jerked the wheel, nearly flipping them as he turned onto a street. He accelerated until the engine sounded as if it would blow up. As they approached the fence that surrounded the World's Largest PX and the Hotel Three complex, he slammed on the brakes, locking the wheels.

Santini was nearly thrown from the seat. He caught himself at the last moment. then stared at the fat sergeant. "Thanks."

"You tell your Major Madden I don't appreciate being called out to haul some sergeant around."

Santini felt his blood boil. The fat sergeant probably spent the day in some air-conditioned motor pool office pretending to work while he read Playboy when he wasn't making life miserable for everyone around him.

"I'll be happy to inform the major of your attitude. Maybe he'll have General Carson call down and see about arranging a transfer."

"You do that," said the sergeant.

Santini knew the sergeant knew that Carson would never call. He reached into the back, grabbed his gear and climbed out of the jeep. He didn't say another word to the man.

At the Hotel Three terminal he found there were six helicopters sitting on the pads, none of them cranked. Entering the terminal, a wooden structure at the base of the tower where the scheduling took place, he found five men ignoring the room's sole woman. She was wearing jungle fatigues with captain's bars pinned to the collar and a pair of scissors thrust through the pen loop of her pocket flap. It meant she was a nurse.

Santini wondered why none of the men were talking to her. She was a small, pretty woman with short dark hair and big eyes. He moved to the counter opposite the door and leaned against it. It was made of plywood and had been painted green at one time. There was a tired Spec Four working back there.

"I need to get to Moc Hoa," said Santini.

"Good luck," said the specialist.

"You have anything going out in that area?"

The specialist turned and looked at the scheduling board. It was a huge white piece of plywood covered with plastic. Grease pencil notes and the names and numbers of helicopters, along with their destinations and their takeoff times, were scribbled across it.

"Got some guy from the Crusaders who said he'd be flying out there in about fifteen minutes. That's the best I can do, and you'll have to talk to the AC. Maybe he'll give you a lift to Moc Hoa, or maybe he'll just tell you to go fuck yourself and leave you here."

"Pencil in my name," said Santini.

When that was completed he moved over to the lounge area, which took up one side of the building and contained some beat-up, faded furniture. There were dozens of magazines scattered around, most missing covers. Ashtrays were filled with cigarette butts, and the dirty concrete floor was covered with more butts.

Santini stopped and surveyed the area again. The nurse was reading a paperback novel while the five men stole glances at her. Two of them talked in low tones and then laughed. Something had happened before he had arrived that had separated the men from the woman, but he decided he wasn't interested in finding out what it was.

He moved over and sat down in a chair close to the nurse. As he did so, she glanced up at him, at his green beret and then at his weapon. Then she turned her attention back to her book.

Santini checked his equipment again and wished he had brought a book with him. Instead, he studied the nurse; there weren't many round-eyed women in Vietnam. He could tell she had tailored fatigues because they fitted her better than a normal issue uniform would.

She glanced up at him, and Santini smiled. She returned it briefly, politely, then resumed reading before he could say anything. He thought her attitude was silly, but he could understand it. Given the slightest encouragement, ninety percent of the men would pounce, and she would be busy fighting off another advance.

A pilot, dressed in jungle fatigues and wearing a pistol in an old West holster, entered and talked to the specialist. He glanced over at Santini and moved toward him.

"You need a ride to Moc Hoa?"

Santini got to his feet and nodded. "Yes, sir. It's rather critical I get there."

"Grab your gear and I'll see what I can do. At the worst, I'll get you closer, maybe Tay Ninh. There's a Special Forces camp at Tay Ninh West where I can drop you off if I can't get you all the way to Moc Hoa."

"I really need to get to Moc Hoa."

"Well, we'll have to wait until we get out of here. I'll have to coordinate with my operations in Tay Ninh, but I don't think it'll be a problem, though we're getting pretty high on blade time."

"Blade time?"

The pilot grinned and wiped an eye with his finger. "Ah, yes, blade time. A new and delightful concept dreamed up by the bureaucrats to keep track of how much flying the helicopters do. They don't want to overstress the machines. We have to be careful of them. Pilots, they don't care about, but by God, we'd better not fly the helicopters more than six hours a day."

"Do they get tired?"

The pilot shrugged. "Who knows? Maybe they have a better union than WOPA."

"What's a wopa?"

"Warrant Officer Protective Association. Listen, we better get moving."

Santini turned and picked up his gear. Then, seeing that the nurse was watching, he couldn't help himself. "It's been fun. Don't forget to write."

She laughed but didn't say anything.

Santini caught up to the pilot at the scheduling board. The pilot held up a hand. "I've got one more passenger." He turned and shouted, "Captain Packer?"

The nurse closed her book and stood. As she picked up her kit, she said, "Yes."

"Ready to go."

She grabbed the bag near her chair and moved toward them. Santini couldn't believe his luck, though he had no idea what he would be able to do with it. A helicopter wasn't the place to start a romance.

As they crossed to the door, one of the men shouted, "Hope you rot, bitch!"

Outside Santini asked, "What did you do to them?"

She glanced at him. "They wanted to get real friendly real fast and I wasn't interested. They thought I should allow them to do whatever they wanted because they're real soldiers, you see."

"Oh." He looked over his shoulder and saw two of them standing in the doorway. He wished he'd paid more attention to them while he was inside, because he was sure they were nothing more than garrison troopers—men who sat around the base camps and did paperwork and made life miserable for the soldiers who had to hump through the bush. They probably weren't real soldiers. At least he hoped they weren't. He hoped that real soldiers would have more class than that and would have respected the woman's privacy.

They reached the chopper and climbed in. They sat together on the troop seat, but Santini refused to speak first. He wanted her to begin the conversation, but she seemed to be unaware of him. And then it was too late because the pilot had cranked the engine and the whine from the turbine overwhelmed all sound around them.

A few moments later they lifted off and climbed out. They turned west, above the lights of Saigon, and flew out over the blackness that was the Vietnamese landscape. Santini watched the ground through the open cargo compartment door. There were varying shades of gray that marked roads or canals and once, through the mist and the patches of low-hanging clouds, he saw the lights that defined Cu Chi.

The crew chief reached around and tapped Santini on the shoulder. He leaned closer, pulling the boom mike on his helmet out of the way, and shouted, "AC said we'll be able to take you on to Moc Hoa. Weather's closing in on us, but right now we can make it. He may have to divert into Tay Ninh if it gets much worse out there. Tay Ninh has a GCI, so the weather has to be real lousy to keep us out of there."

Santini nodded in an exaggerated motion and yelled back, "Tell him thanks and that I owe him one. I appreciate the effort even if we don't make it to Moc Hoa."

As he turned back he felt something press against his foot, then realized it was the nurse's foot. He kept his foot where it was, slightly under the troop seat, and wondered what he should say or if he should push back to let her know that he knew. There had to be something for him to do or say, but after what she had told him about the incident in the terminal, he couldn't think of anything witty. So he sat there, her foot pressed against his.

The chopper banked once, and she fell against him. When it righted, it seemed that she hesitated a moment longer than necessary before sitting up again. He knew she was flirting with him and he didn't understand it completely, not after what she had told him about the other soldiers and their attitudes.

Then she shifted around and he saw both her feet. That made no sense because he could still feel her foot pressing his. He glanced down and realized he was playing footsie with one of the braces on the troop seat. He laughed at himself and sat back to enjoy the rest of the flight.

Finally they reached Moc Hoa and landed. The weather had deteriorated until they had been flying at under five hundred feet, the helicopter darting in and out of the low-hanging clouds. Through the windshield he could see the weather was getting worse. Soon it would be too bad for even the helicopters.

As the skids touched the ground, a jeep appeared. Santini pulled his equipment toward him and unbuckled his seat belt. As he moved, he felt Packer's hand on his. She grinned and said, "Hey, don't forget to write."

Santini shrugged and dropped to the ground. As soon as he was clear, the chopper leaped into the air. When it was gone and they were wrapped in a deafening silence, the driver of the jeep said, "Looks like it's tonight."

"Shit," said Santini.

7

SPECIAL FORCES CAMP
A-337, PLEI SOI

Fulton stood in the command post, a mike in one hand and a map in the other. A lantern burned on the table-top, throwing its bright white light into the corner. Fulton had laid his weapon on the table and set his helmet next to it. The sound of the mortars and rockets and the rattle of the small-arms fire told him the assault hadn't started yet. Not with the mortar shells still falling.

He was having difficulty with the communications; there was a lot of static pop and buzz on the radio as the storm moved east. The voices faded so that he couldn't hear. He keyed the mike. "Say again. You're coming in broken and garbled."

"Roger. Be advised that the . . ."

Fulton waited, but the voice didn't come back. He glanced at Hampton, the junior communications NCO. "We have a land line to Tay Ninh?"

"That went about an hour ago. I figure Charlie either cut it outside the camp or one of the mortars got it."

Fulton flipped the mike at him. "Well, get this damned thing working. Tell Winger at Moc Hoa that we want the Mike Force on standby and see about arranging airlift for them. Oh, and coordinate with the Air Force for some fighter support in here.''

''Weather's going to cause us some real grief,'' said Hampton.

''Right now that's the least of our problems. I'm going to the FCT and see if anything's happening. If you get through, give me a shout on the field phone.''

Fulton grabbed his weapon and helmet and ran up the stairs. He stopped at the doorway, just as two mortar rounds landed inside the compound. Then he sprinted to the base of the tower. He crouched there and looked up the ladder. It seemed to stretch upward into infinity, making him wonder if he could reach the top before a sniper picked him off. Rather than worry about it, though, he slung his rifle, stood and grabbed a rung. But the crash of an exploding round inside the redoubt made him flinch. He hesitated, then practically ran up the ladder, diving over the sandbags. When he got to his feet, he turned and grinned at Minh and Timmons. ''What's the situation here?''

Minh pointed to the north. ''We've seen quite a bit of activity in that direction, old boy. Mortar tubes and occasional flashes of light. Charlie is massing in that area. To the west, same sort of thing, but that's probably a diversion. Real assault will come from the north.''

All three of them ducked as heavy machine gun rounds smashed into the sandbags around the tower. They could feel the impact of the bullets slamming into the tower, throwing dirt over them.

''What the shit was that?'' Fulton rasped.

Minh looked over the top of the sandbags. ''Something new has been added. Those are probably twelve-sevens. I didn't see the muzzle-flashes.'' He looked at the men with him. ''Anyone see them?''

''No.''

Fulton rubbed his face, now wet with the mist that was all that remained of the rain. He felt tired. His body ached and he wanted to sleep. ''What do you make of it?''

''I believe, old boy, that we're going to have a major assault on the camp sometime in the next hour. You'd better get on the horn and alert everyone.''

''You sure it's going to be a major assault?''

''Captain Fulton, I've only seen something like this once before,'' said Minh. ''That was just before a regiment hit us at the old Triple Nickel. The bombardment was designed to destroy as much of the camp as possible. Within minutes they'll send in the sappers.''

''All right, Captain Minh,'' said Fulton. ''I'm going back to the command post and see if we can get some help in here.''

''I'd suggest you hurry.''

''CAPTAIN,'' SAID FETTERMAN, ''I think we've got movement in the wire.''

Gerber grabbed a pair of binoculars, held them to his eyes and demanded, ''Where?''

Fetterman moved closer, being careful not to silhouette himself in the firing port. ''About a hundred meters out and at one o'clock.''

''Okay,'' said Gerber, turning his binoculars toward the area Fetterman had pointed out. He swept the ground carefully, but the mist was too thick and the night too dark.

''Can't see anything,'' said Gerber. ''Tell you what. Why don't you break out your M-79 and put a couple of rounds of willie pete out there? See if that stirs up anything.''

Fetterman moved to the rear of the small bunker and grabbed the M-79. Using his fingers, he located the white phosphorus rounds by size and shape and loaded one. He jammed two more into his pocket and returned to the firing port.

''You going to tell anyone we're shooting?''

''Right.'' Gerber found the handset for the field phone, spun the crank and told the command post they would be putting out three rounds of willie pete.

Then Fetterman adjusted the sight, aimed and fired. A second later there was an explosion in the wire as the round detonated into a brilliant fountain of flaming white. The ground was brightly illuminated for a moment until the willie pete burned itself out.

Gerber used his binoculars again. Behind the flaming debris he thought he saw a human shape, but the mist made it impossible to tell.

Fetterman fired a second round, dropping this one just beyond the first. Part of the eastern end of the bunker line opened fire, their rounds churning up the ground near the wire where Fetterman had aimed. Red tracers flashed into the night, some of them tumbling.

And then there was a single searing note from a bugle, and it seemed that the wire blew up. There were five explosions, one following the other, walking toward the bunker line as gaps appeared.

Gerber grabbed his rifle and flipped the safety off. ''This is it,'' he said.

The Browning M-2 .50-caliber machine gun sited against the far wall of the bunker opened fire with a slow, monotonous hammering. The hot brass ejected from it rattled against the wood of the bunker, and the muzzle-flash reached out nearly ten feet.

From outside came a rising shout, and trip flares began to go off as the enemy started the ground assault. They rushed from the safety of the trees half a klick away, materializing out of the mist, screaming and shouting. They fired as they ran, ignoring the booby traps and trip flares scattered through the wire.

Gerber snatched at the handset of the field phone and pressed the switch at its center. "Here they come. Give us illumination over the north wall."

He tossed the handset away and aimed his rifle out the firing port. He saw a man loom out of the grayness of the mist as the first of the flares popped overhead. Gerber fired quickly and saw the man go down. The enemy soldier raised himself slightly and then collapsed, lying still.

Around him the others were beginning to shout. At first he could hear the individual reports of the weapons reverberating off the walls in the confined space. Then the sound grew until it was a single, low roar like thunder in the distance, punctuated by the hammering of the .50-caliber machine gun and the detonations of grenades.

Bugles pierced the night, their calls high and wild like the roars of beasts hunting in the jungle. There were whistles and shouts and screams. Green tracers appeared in the darkness, looking like glowing softballs.

The enemy wavered at the third strand of wire. The ground was bright with flares raining down around them. The strikers in the bunkers were pouring heavy fire into them. At the same time, the grenades and booby traps exploded, killing them.

A few fell to the ground, returning fire. They burned through their magazines rapidly, trying to force the

Americans and the Vietnamese strikers to keep their heads down.

Fetterman switched from willie pete to HE in the M-79. He cranked off a round, saw it land among the men in the wire and began pumping the shells through the weapon as fast as he could load and fire it.

Gerber was firing on full-auto, raking the ground outside the bunker. When one magazine was empty, he dropped it on the floor and snatched another from the pile to his right. The American mortar crews kept the illumination coming so that the wire was lighted with a strange, shifting light from the flares oscillating under their chutes.

Suddenly a single searing blast blotted out everything around it. Dirt and debris rained down, and the cloud it created hid the enemy. The firing from the VC and NVA tapered to an occasional round and then halted completely.

Gerber emptied his magazine into the dirt cloud. When his weapon stopping firing, he changed magazines quickly and ordered, "Cease fire! Cease fire!"

Fetterman popped open his M-79, letting the smoke blow from the hot barrel. He kicked the empty casings away from his feet so he wouldn't stumble on them later. "Not much of an attack."

"They were just taking out the wire. They've made themselves some good gaps in it now. Next assault will bring them to the bunker line."

"Yeah," agreed Fetterman. "I think it might be time to abandon the bunkers."

"Let's wait and see if they drop any more mortars on us. If not, we'll set up behind the bunker."

"Captain, I think we maybe should coordinate with Fulton."

"If he wants us, he knows where we are." Gerber reached down and seized the field phone, dragging it toward the bunker entrance, taking care he didn't rip the wires free. He set it down and crawled out. Coming to his feet behind a low sandbag wall, he surveyed the field in front of him. Dark shapes that were the bodies of the enemy killed in the assault, lay scattered in the wire. He made a mental note of the gaps in the wire. The next assault would easily reach the bunker line, just as he had told Fetterman.

SANTINI STOOD in the commo bunker watching the NCO there handle the radios and relay the calls from Camp A-337 to various facilities, including the arty control, the Air Force in Saigon and the Twenty-fifth Infantry Third Brigade Headquarters at Dau Tieng.

The sergeant put down one of the mikes and said, "Captain Fulton reports that the enemy is in the wire now, but they beat off the assault. He's requesting a Medevac."

"What's the weather like?"

"I'm afraid it's so bad we won't be able to get a flight of choppers in there. The Medevac is a different story. Something might be arranged, but other than that they're on their own until morning. We can send out a rescue column then."

Santini moved closer. "That's what Charlie wants. He'll ambush the column."

"Hell, Sergeant, we all know that. We'll use an armor spearhead and have gun support."

"That's not what I mean."

"It'll draw pressure off the men in the camp."

"But we need to do something now," said Santini. "Helicopters could put our Mike Force on the ground right where Fulton needs them."

"It's the damn weather," the sergeant said. "It keeps the choppers on the ground. They try to come in low in the rain at night and it's going to be the biggest disaster since the Little Big Horn."

Santini sighed. "Where's the B-team commander or the Mike Force CO?"

"Probably in the club."

"Thanks." Santini took the steps up two at a time and found himself standing in the wet night. Rain, which had been reported at A-337, now threatened them, effectively grounding all the choppers. There was no way they could run a combat assault at night in the rain.

For a moment he stood staring at the black clouds that hid the moon and stars. The Air Force couldn't run an air strike in this weather, either, at least not a close air support mission. If Fulton or Gerber knew where the enemy was rallying, they might be able to disperse them. But if the enemy was storming the wire, the Air Force was blind, too.

He turned, strolling along the wooden boardwalk until he came to the officers' club. He took off his beret and stood in the doorway, an anxious look on his face. The club was a dimly lit, flimsy wooden building with bamboo matting on the walls and floor. It had a huge bar at one end, and an old jukebox was shoved into a corner. There were rattan tables and chairs and each table had a small candle on it. Captured weapons decorated the walls, and two floor fans stood in opposite corners, blowing warm, moist air at each other.

Santini spotted the men he'd come to find and approached their table. He slipped into the empty chair and said, "Sorry to bother you, sir, but the enemy is in the wire at Plei Soi."

"And what do you want me to do?"

"Let's get the Mike Force ready to move out," suggested Santini.

The major scratched the back of his neck. "Why should we do that? Has Fulton called for help yet?"

"No, sir, but he's going to need it. We won't be able to get air support in there with the weather the way it is."

"Sergeant . . ."

"Santini, sir."

"Sergeant Santini, I'm not inclined to stir up trouble at this end unless Captain Fulton requests it. He knows what's going on at that camp of his. If he asks for help, then we'll see what we can do."

"Yes, sir," said Santini. "I just didn't think we should wait until the last minute. Hell, sir, we don't even have the choppers here."

"No, and we won't get them unless we have an immediate mission. No one is going to let ten, twelve helicopters sit on the ground doing nothing. Besides, the weather is so lousy that not much is going to be airborne tonight."

"But—"

"Look, Sergeant, I understand your concern, but we're not just sitting here doing nothing. Mike Force is on alert. They're standing by in their hootches, in uniform with their equipment right beside them. Helicopter crews at Tay Ninh and Cu Chi are on alert and are in their aircraft. Your own Major Madden arranged that and then coordinated through us. Now until Captain Fulton calls for help, we're not going to start shifting troops all around the AO."

"Yes, sir."

FETTERMAN WAS STANDING behind the bunker, leaning forward slightly with both elbows propped on the sandbags, binoculars to his eyes. ''I've got some movement out there.''

Then, as if to lend credence to his words, there was a building of bugle calls and whistles. Firing erupted in the darkness, the muzzle-flashes of the enemy weapons lost in the mist that hung over the camp. As the enemy force began to take shape in the grayness, the last of the wire exploded and the Vietcong poured through as if someone had opened floodgates.

Gerber checked the magazine on his weapon and then jacked a round into the chamber. For an instant he considered entering the bunker again, but decided against it. With the enemy coming in force, he didn't want to be trapped in a bunker. He wanted to be outside where he could move around.

The VC raced through the gaps in the wire, threw ladders across the punji moat and began scrambling across it. Gerber opened fire then. A tracer round blew past the head of an enemy soldier, frightening him. The man instinctively ducked, lost his balance and fell into the moat. He emitted a blood-curdling shriek as the punji stakes pierced his body.

The firing intensified, but the VC didn't hesitate this time. They scrambled up the earthen embankment that marked the perimeter of the camp, and engaged the defenders. Gerber shot the first three men he saw. Their bodies tumbled back out of sight. And then there were too many of them too close to him.

Gerber leaped toward them and swung his rifle like a baseball bat. The light plastic stock clipped one man, knocking him to the side. Gerber spun, faced a new adversary, but the enemy grabbed the barrel of the rifle, twisting it. Gerber let go, stepped forward and kicked at the man's crotch. He felt his foot connect and felt the flesh and bone give. The VC fell, screaming. He pivoted and kicked again, his foot snapping the man's head back, killing him.

Gerber scooped the AK from the mud. Afraid to fire it, he extended the bayonet. As he did, the first soldier came at him again, and Gerber tore open the man's throat with the bayonet. The Vietcong screamed as the blood poured from his damaged body. With both hands on his neck trying to stop the bleeding, he fell to the ground.

A third VC appeared in front of him, and Gerber knocked the soldier's barrel away, thrusting at him. The bayonet penetrated the man's side, but he didn't seem to feel it. He twisted his body, and as the blade came free he leaped at Gerber. The Special Forces captain tried to use his weapon, but the two men fell into the mud.

Gerber rolled and came up first. He punched out, his force concentrated on the heel of his hand as the palm connected with the VC's sternum. There was a sickening crack of bone, and the man died as his heart was destroyed.

Before he could move, another attacker knocked Gerber over. He clawed at his holster, jerking the Browning 9 mm free and flipping off the safety. He fired, the muzzle-flash licking out to touch the side of the man's head. As it exploded, there was a groan from the man's lips. He died as he fell.

Gerber rolled away and got to his knees. He saw Fetterman holding off two of the enemy with his bayonet. He grinned as he shot one of them and yelled, "That's one you owe me."

Then he was too busy to worry about it. He scrambled to the right so that the bunker was at his back. His hands were shaking as he tried to kill a sapper running across the compound. He fired again and again and finally the man fell, rolling once. Rather than worry about his wound, the enemy tried to cover his satchel charge. As his fingers touched the straps of the pack, there was an explosion that knocked everyone to the ground. The VC disappeared in a flash of light and fire.

Gerber dropped the magazine from his pistol and slammed a new one home. He chambered a round and then wiped a hand across his wet face. As he climbed to his feet, he saw another soldier reach the top of the earthen barricade. The enemy leaped at Gerber, who raised his weapon and fired. The round caught the VC in the chest, but the impact didn't stop him. He hurled himself at Gerber, who sidestepped. As the man hit the ground, Gerber dropped a knee on the middle of his back, pinning him in the muck. He pushed the barrel of the pistol into the base of the VC's neck and shot him once. He felt the man's body spasm in death.

On his feet again, he saw two men running toward the fire control tower. Gerber spread his feet and squeezed off the rounds. One man went down in a sprawling heap, but the other tossed his satchel charge at the base of the tower. When he turned, Gerber put a round through his chest, killing him.

ROBIN MORROW STOOD AT THE WINDOWS that looked out on downtown Saigon, watching as the rain finally came. At first it was a drizzle that barely got the streets wet and then it was a downpour that threatened to wash away the South Vietnamese capital. A smile played at her lips as the Vietnamese girls in their light blouses and short skirts at first ignored the rain and then fled to the cover of doorways and overhangs. The GIs, on a night's pass, most of them soaking wet, chased after the girls.

Morrow turned as the rain began to eat through the crust of dirt and oil smeared on the windows, making the colors of the neon signs run together. There were only a few reporters in the city room, and no one was working. Two were playing cards, slapping them down and laughing a lot. Another sat reading a *Time* magazine while the last sat near a tiny black-and-white portable television, engrossed in a program from AFVN.

Morrow crossed the floor and pulled a chair close to the man with the TV. "What's on, Ed?"

"A year-old special with Dean Martin," he replied. "I saw this last time I was in the States. But it beats watching Brian and Vincent play cards."

"Seems pretty dead," said Morrow, nodding toward the TV set.

Ed misunderstood her and said, "I haven't seen Vietnam this quiet since the Gulf of Tonkin. It's as if the enemy has all disappeared or lost the will to fight."

"You think it means the war is about to end?" asked Morrow, not really believing it herself.

Ed shifted so that he could look at her. He reached over and turned off the sound on the TV. "That's what's puzzling me. I've been here off and on for a couple of years and I haven't seen a time like this. The Vietcong are usually doing something, even if it's only a couple of mortar rounds dropped on a Green Beret camp. We're not even getting that. Casualty figures and reports of contact are way down."

"That's good for us, isn't it?"

"If you mean for us, as the United States, the answer is yes, it's very good. It'll mean we can get our soldiers out of here and stop spending a billion dollars a year. If you mean good for us as journalists, then the answer is no. Without this war, there aren't any big ongoing stories. I mean, you send a new reporter here, some kid fresh out of school, and he can cut his teeth, make a reputation for himself in a year. Without the war, without the constant strain of fresh stories, that kid will spend years trying to build a career and might never make it.''

"Maybe the enemy is planning something big." She had nothing to base that on except that Gerber was gone and there were some uneasy people over at MACV. But then, there were always uneasy people over at MACV. Besides, it was the hopeful note that Ed would want: the war wasn't winding down.

"Can't see it," said Ed. "Vietcong don't have the forces for any major operations. They're a guerilla army who are only effective in hit-and-run operations. They just can't field a force much larger than a regiment or two. No, I'm afraid this story has just about run its course."

Morrow remembered Gerber talking about divisions. "What about the divisions that are reported? That would seem to indicate large numbers of enemy forces."

Ed snorted. "Those are paper numbers. Our Army learns that a couple of VC regiments are in the area and they label it a division. It's just not the same as the twelve or fifteen thousand men that make up one of our divisions." Ed rocked back in his chair and laced his hands behind his head. "No, I'm afraid the war here is almost over. The enemy doesn't exist, and we're going to have to find ourselves some other beat to cover because this one is dead."

Morrow glanced at the TV screen and then at Ed. He seemed to have everything under control, seemed to

understand everything there was to understand about
the war in Vietnam. He had been here longer than anyone she knew, except Gerber and Fetterman, and neither of them actually talked about the war with her. They
mentioned what they had been doing in general terms,
but they never talked about the big picture. Maybe it was
because they didn't understand the big picture as well
as someone on the outside. Someone like Ed, whose
whole existence didn't seem to reflect combat and the
war. Maybe he knew what he was talking about.

Again she looked at him as he reached to turn up the
sound on the TV. There was a smug look on his face.
Maybe he really did have his finger on the pulse of the
war. Maybe. But somehow she didn't think he did. She
thought he was full of shit.

IN THE FIRE CONTROL TOWER Captain Minh watched
the fight as it developed on the north wall. He had seen
the feint against the west wall pushed back almost before it could start and had seen the attack on the east
halted before it could penetrate the third strand of wire.

But then, on the north, the enemy had come boiling
out of the gray mist, hurdled the punji pit almost as if it
didn't exist and then were on top of the earthen embankment. Gerber and the strikers there had leaped to
meet the threat in hand-to-hand fighting.

Minh used his rifle, aiming at the men still outside the
barricade, picking them off one by one. He dropped a
couple into the punji pit and hit two more as they reached
the top of the earthwork barricade. And when the
strikers and Americans became too mixed for him, he
began searching for targets still in the wire outside the
camp.

All the time that Minh was firing, Lopez was on the field phone directing the mortar fire. The 81s kept the illumination burning over the north wall so that the night took on a strange gray-white light and the attackers became dark shapes moving like the ghosts of some deserted ship.

Lopez was also running the 60 mm mortars, coordinating the firing there so that the rounds dropped among the enemy, hitting both the north and east walls. He sat with his back against the sandbags, peeking over the top to watch the detonations and then dropping back to give new coordinates to the men in the mortar pits.

Minh fell to the floor as machine gun fire raked the tin roof, snapping through it. He glanced up at the new holes, reloaded his empty weapons, then popped up.

Below him one man ran toward the tower, but fell with a bullet in the leg. He tried to scramble toward his satchel, but it exploded with a roar that shook the tower. Shrapnel rattled against the roof, and the smoke from the detonation engulfed the tower, obscuring their view.

Minh wiped the dirt and mud from his face. A smoking crater, ten feet across, was only thirty feet from the tower. And then, out of the confusion on the north wall, more sappers appeared. One of them was cut down, but the other threw his charge at the legs of the tower.

''Get down!'' shouted Minh, grabbing a post.

The explosion rattled Minh's teeth and made it hard for him to see. He felt the heat wash over him, felt the fire sting his face as the charge detonated and the heat rolled up the side of the tower. Surprised that he was still alive, he noticed the tower was still upright. He grabbed the top of the sandbag wall and hauled himself to his feet.

Before he could shout again, the tower began to lean. It fell slowly, as if someone were trying to hold it up. The sandbags shifted, tumbling toward Minh, pinning him to the side as the tower hit the ground.

8

FIFTH SPECIAL FORCES HEADQUARTERS, NHA TRANG

Madden sat in the commo bunker before the racks of radios, which were shoved into one corner. The indicators glowed red and green, and he watched the needles of the yellow VU meters bounce as the radio traffic came in. He seized the mic when he heard his call sign.

"This is Werewolf. Go."

"Roger, Werewolf. I have the Mike Force ready and understand that Diablo Six is under assault."

"You are a go," said Madden.

"Verbal authorization is needed at this end from MACV" came the reply.

"Christ," said Madden. He lifted the mike and added, "Authorization will be coming." He tossed the mike to the NCO who stood there and told him, "I want a land line to MACV headquarters, General Davidson."

The NCO shrugged and took a deep breath. He sat down at the switchboard that was a conglomeration of different parts: mismatched wires and commo equipment that had been created slowly as the American presence in Vietnam had grown. Now it was a night-mare.

The sergeant wiped his hands on his thighs, then gingerly reached up like a scientist about to awaken the sleeping monster. He pulled a wire, plugged it in, reached over and cranked a handle. He heard a distant voice and was told the lines were down between Nha Trang and Saigon.

"Shit," said the sergeant. He began to jury-rig a connection from Nha Trang to Ban Me Thuot to Da Lat to Phan Rang to Phan Thiet to Bien Hoa to Cu Chi to Saigon. The voice at the far end was small, tinny and quiet, but it was articulate. The sergeant handed the handset to Madden.

"Major Madden here. I'd like to speak with General Davidson." He waited and then shouted, "Madden for General Davidson."

He fell silent, nodded, then yelled, "Yes, it's important. Get him on the phone."

Madden lifted the phone so that he could listen, but the mike was around his eyes. He looked at the sergeant who was sitting in the half-light of the bunker, reading a copy of *Newsweek*. He was paying no attention to Madden.

Madden turned to face the map fastened to the wall. He stepped forward to take a closer look. There was a large red circle in the area of Camp A-337. Studying it, northwest of the Angel's Wing and just south of Hoa Hiep, he could see where the Ho Chi Minh Trail crossed the border into South Vietnam. The camp had been well situated.

The tinny voice said, "Davidson here. This had better be important."

"This is Madden in Nha Trang, General. We have a situation developing to the west and need authorization to commit." Madden realized he wasn't telling the general much, but he didn't trust the lima lima any more than he trusted the radio.

Over the phone he heard, "You have the authorization you need, but only from Moc Hoa."

"Understood."

"If more is needed, you'll have to coordinate through here."

"Understood," repeated Madden. "Thank you, General." He gave the handset back to the NCO. He moved to the radio, took the mike and said, "Epsilon, this is Werewolf Six."

"Go, Six."

"You have permission to begin. Authorization comes from the highest levels. Verbal confirmation available at MACV."

"Roger. Understood."

AT MOC HOA, Santini handed the mike to the communications specialist and said, "Thanks."

He ran out of the bunker and headed back to the club. He found both officers still sitting in the same place. "We've got the authorization to go, sir."

Colonel Brucchard slammed the table with his hand. "Who in hell told you to go for authorization?"

"No one, Colonel. I knew what the situation was and thought I'd better clear the decks."

"Jesus Christ. I don't know what the Army is coming to." He looked at Major Winger. "These NCOs are beginning to believe that crap about running the Army." He turned back to Santini. "Okay, Sergeant. I have a question for you. Now that you have the authorization, how do you plan to move the Mike Force from here to Camp A-337?''

"We'll need airlift."

"I told you it's unavailable. Weather's inhibiting it."

"Then trucks," said Santini.

"Sergeant, this isn't your concern. We're fully aware of the situation at Plei Soi and don't need constant updates from you. Major Winger and I are engaged in an important high-level meeting now. Besides, there's nothing we can do until first light."

Santini took a deep breath and stared at the two men. He couldn't believe they were sitting there, playing cards and drinking beer, unconcerned about the attack on Fulton's camp. He wanted to grab one of them and punch him.

Finally one of the officers looked up at him. "Sergeant Santini, we have everything arranged. The vehicles we need are here at the camp. But there's no airlift, not in this weather. Now I'll have one of my officers confirm the authorization in Saigon. It's not that I don't believe you, but if something goes wrong, it's my butt in a sling."

Santini realized that everything was done. Neither officer had felt the need to explain the situation to him because he wasn't a member of their unit and wasn't involved in the planning of the mission. It was now up to them as to when and how they deployed the Mike Force. He looked from one to the other and said, "I'd like permission to accompany the Mike Force when it's deployed."

"You may stand by in their area."

"Thank you, sir." Santini turned and headed out of the club, feeling like an idiot.

THE ENEMY ASSAULT had broken as they'd climbed the earthen embankment. A few of the Vietcong had gotten inside the camp and a couple had used their satchel charges, but then the firing had become too intense and the enemy had fled before they could inflict any real casualties. Gerber stood with his head down, his Browning in his right hand, looking at the body of the man he had just killed. He was a young Vietnamese who wore black shorts and a black shirt with a bloodstained chest pouch for extra AK magazines. His boots looked like high-top tennis shoes, and the blood on his face was mixed in with the mud that stained his clothes.

Gerber was breathing hard, staring at the dead man as the shooting from the M-16s, M-1s and AKs slowed until it was a sporadic rattle. He stood staring at the man, not because he was the first Gerber had killed, but because he was the most recent.

Gerber turned and looked at the bunker line. There were bodies sprawled along it, some of them in American fatigues, some of them in the khaki of the NVA and the rest in the black pajamas of the VC. Weapons were lying around them. Broken knives and rifles were strewn about. Packs and entrenching tools, along with other equipment, lay scattered everywhere.

Gerber moved toward the bunker and crouched there. In the wires were more dead. He could hear a couple of the enemy soldiers crying for help.

He felt a hand on his shoulder and saw Fetterman.

"You okay, Captain?"

"Fine. You?"

"I'm okay. What's next?"

"Well, I think they're going to be encouraged. They got into the camp this time. We can expect the real push now."

Before Fetterman could respond, a figure loomed out of the dark behind them and then crouched near them. Fulton took a moment to catch his breath. "We've got a Medevac coming in."

"You sure that's a good idea, Captain?" asked Fetterman.

"No choice. We've got some badly wounded men who need to get out of here or they're going to die soon."

"What do you need from us?"

Fulton looked at the damaged bunker line, then at the dead men. His gaze strayed to the fields to the north. "When the chopper comes in, we've got to keep the enemy busy and give it good covering fire. It'll be in and out in less than a minute."

"Where is it going to land?"

Fulton turned and looked back toward the redoubt. "I'm going to try to put it down in the open area between the east side of the bunker line and the gate of the redoubt. That way, while it's sitting on the ground, it'll be relatively safe from enemy small-arms fire."

"How long until it arrives?"

"Five minutes at the outside. Keep your ears open, and when you hear something, you'll need to start pumping out rounds to protect the chopper."

"Will do," said Gerber.

Fulton turned and ran back toward the redoubt. After he disappeared, Fetterman said, "I'll alert the men in the corner so they can cover."

Moments later the first of the telltale pops of rotor blades reached Gerber's ears. He looked south, but there were only clouds and the glowing of flares that began to wink out one by one. Fulton had shut off the artillery for a moment to give the helicopter a chance to get in.

When it was dark, with light from only a few scattered fires, Gerber got to his feet and ran to the right. He stopped at the corner of the perimeter and waited until Fetterman came out of the bunker.

"They're ready. Just waiting for us to give them the word," Fetterman said.

The sound of the chopper got louder, penetrating the rattle of the small-arms fire around the camp. And then it began to fade, as if the pilot had thought better of the mission. Gerber listened until it was gone. He glanced at Fetterman, little more than a dim outline, and shrugged.

And then the sound came again, this time from the west and to the south. It was low, as if the chopper was near the ground. Gerber knew the pilot was making a serious attempt to reach the camp. Keeping his eyes on the sky to the south, where the sound came from, he reached out and tapped Fetterman on the shoulder. "Have them open fire," he said. "Have them open fire with everything now."

As the strikers began to shoot, Gerber moved to the east behind one of the bunkers. In the south, over the edge of the camp, he could just make out a dark shape. It rushed toward him, the sound beginning to overwhelm.

The chopper flared, the nose coming up as it rolled over on its side. Gerber was hit by a blast of wind as the helicopter righted itself. As the skids leveled, the chopper slipped to the ground.

On touchdown, two men carrying a stretcher ran from the redoubt. They lifted it up, and one of the crewmen in the aircraft grabbed the end. When the stretcher was loaded, two more men ran out, helping a third. As that man was climbing aboard, another stretcher team came out. A limping man hobbled from the redoubt, and a crewman helped him into the chopper. Someone stepped up on the skid so that he could say something to the pilot, and as he dropped back to the ground, the aircraft picked up to a hover.

Firing came from outside the camp again. Dozens of machine guns, both RPDs and the heavier twelve-sevens, began to pump a steady stream of fire into the camp. All the strikers began to shoot.

The Medevac chopper spun as if on pole, and the nose dipped. The aircraft began racing for the end of the perimeter, picking up speed and then gaining altitude. Gerber lost sight of it in the gloom and the mist, but he could hear the rotor blades snapping and the engine roaring.

The enemy seemed to suddenly realize what had happened. Firing on the east and south increased. Emerald tracers reached into the sky. Bright green lines were drawn, each moving toward the helicopter. Some of them struck, disappearing into the thin skin of the fuselage.

The aircraft seemed to tremble in the air. Its path was no longer straight. It wobbled, dived and then came up again. It steadied itself and begin a charging dive at the ground as if to pick up speed. Flames blossomed near the engine and dripped down the side. The fire grew, spreading back along the tail boom, seeming to engulf it.

The door guns continued to fire, pouring out ruby tracers as the green ones flashed in. More of them hit, and the helicopter suddenly leaped upward, as if trying to gain the protection of the clouds. And then, as the fires on it seemed to go out for a moment, the aircraft exploded into a flaming orange ball that rained debris into the wire south of the camp.

For an instant it was as if everything had stopped. All eyes were on the glowing ball of fire that continued to climb and then plunged to the ground. The flames reached skyward, almost to the base of the clouds, coloring them yellowish orange.

There was no movement near the burning wreck, and then a smaller, man-sized ball of flame broke free. It took two quick steps before collapsing. As the man died, the flames on the aircraft began to die, too. And then there was a tremendous explosion as the fuel cells detonated, throwing flaming JP-4 and burning metal over the area.

Fetterman stepped close to Gerber and mumbled, "Son of a bitch."

Gerber tore his eyes from the flaming wreckage and looked at Fetterman. "They're going to be coming at us with a vengeance now. They've had a taste of victory."

Fetterman nodded and looked north over the wire that surrounded the camp. The mist was beginning to dissipate, and he could see the jungle nearly three hundred yards away—a black strip where the enemy hid.

There was movement at the very edge of their vision. Gerber heard a single bugle call, and then the tree line erupted.

In seconds the enemy reached the wire and the firing began again. Hundreds of weapons opened up, and their sounds blended into one long explosion. Ruby tracers leaped into the night, crisscrossing with the white and green of the enemy. There were flashes of light as grenades detonated. There were screams and shouts and whistles.

The enemy came quickly, filtering through the gaps in the wire. There was a series of detonations—pops from the exploding C-4 as the last of the claymore mines were fired. A curtain of steel ripped into the enemy, chopping the VC off at the knees, or at the waist, or at the neck. Dozens of them fell, bloodied, mangled messes.

Still the Vietcong kept coming, those in the rear leaping over the dead and dying. They fired their weapons and tossed their grenades. Some were killed by the strikers, others by the last of the booby traps hidden in the wire. They reached the punji pit and crossed it in one quick wave. A few of them fell from the ladders to be impaled on punji stakes.

Gerber fired at a man as he leaped to the top of the earth embankment. As he disappeared, the central bunker exploded. Gerber realized that the VC sappers had finally gotten close enough to toss a satchel charge into it.

The force of the explosion drove Gerber to his knees. He fell on his side, stunned by the detonation. His ears rang from the echoes. He rolled onto his back, his rifle in his hands, and looked up into the grinning face of an NVA soldier. The man thrust forward, trying to plunge his bayonet into Gerber's chest, but the captain blocked the blow with his forearm. The edge of the bayonet sliced through his uniform and his flesh, and he felt a searing pain. He reached out with his other hand and snagged the man's wrist, then brought a knee up, knocking the enemy off-balance. The soldier spun as he fell, landing on his back. Gerber's fist shot out, hitting the VC in the throat, crushing it.

The captain scrambled to his feet and looked at the dying soldier. He shot him once in the chest and then turned to face the rest of the onrushing horde. He fired rapidly until his weapon was empty.

Around him the bunker line was exploding, the structures being methodically destroyed by the VC sappers. Fires burned at both ends of the north wall where the heavy weapons emplacements had been. There were cries of pain, demands for medics and calls for water.

In the wire outside the camp were more of the enemy. It seemed there was an unending supply of them, and as each wave was cut down, a new one appeared. The sound of bugles filled the night, overriding the firing that was tapering off as the two forces became mixed. There were explosions and flashes as both sides threw grenades.

Gerber knew it was no use. They were going to lose the wall. Too many of the enemy had managed to reach it this time. Too many of them had managed to cross the punji pit and climb the earthen barricade.

From somewhere came the command, "Fall back. Fall back."

Gerber ran from the bunker line and leaped the ruins that had been the fire control tower. He dropped behind it and spun, poking his rifle over the rubble and opening fire at the enemy soldiers.

In front of him one man stood holding an M-60 machine gun, a box of ammo at his feet. An unbroken belt of ammo reached to the weapon as the man fired in short bursts, turning as the enemy appeared. Even with the flash suppressor, there was a flame nearly three feet long stabbing into the night, marking his position.

Grenades exploded near him and bullets kicked up mud around him. But his life seemed charmed. He kept pouring fire into the enemy ranks. A dozen Vietcong went down, and still he fired.

Gerber tried to provide covering fire for the machine gunner. He picked off a VC who came up on the gunner's blind side. Gerber shouted at him. "Fall back."

But the man ignored him. Instead he rushed forward, the ammo belt trailing behind in the mud. The belt broke and the weapon jammed. As it did, the VC leaped on the man, slashing at him with their bayonets and knives. When they stood up, Gerber cut them all down with a sustained burst from his weapon.

Then he spotted Fetterman. The sergeant was lying on his back near the smoking ruins of the central bunker. He sat up, threw a grenade at the enemy and dropped back. As soon as the grenade exploded, someone tossed him another and Fetterman went through the procedure once again. He kept it up as the strikers on the bunker line retreated. Some of the strikers tried to disengage in a military fashion, but others simply fled, throwing their weapons away in terror. A few fought a rearguard action, protecting their friends, and died quickly as the enemy overwhelmed them.

Fetterman got his last grenade, pulled the pin and waited. He rolled over, hesitated and then threw the bomb. When it exploded, he scrambled to his feet and began running to the rear. He leaped over the remains of the fire control tower, taking cover behind it.

Gerber glanced at him. "Looks bad for us."

"Yes, sir." Fetterman jammed a fresh magazine into his weapon and opened fire. "We're going to have to get out of here."

"Yeah. I'll cover while you make a run for it."

"Where are we going?"

"Redoubt. Let's hope that Fulton's there."

Fetterman emptied his weapon, ducked and dropped the spent magazine. He jammed another one home and popped up again. The last of the flares burned itself out, and the camp was plunged into darkness. There was flickering firelight from the burning bunkers.

"Go!" yelled Gerber.

Fetterman sprinted until he came to the side of the commo bunker. Then he dropped to the ground and opened fire.

Gerber took off then, running toward him. He dodged right and kept on going until he reached the entrance to the redoubt, where he stopped and turned, firing into the night. Seeing shadows moving near the corner of the perimeter, he shot at them. As he did, Fetterman began to run again.

"Anyone in the commo bunker?" asked Gerber.

"I doubt it, sir. The antennae are all shot to hell and one wall is collapsed."

Three men loomed out of the dark and ran by them. Two more appeared, dragging a wounded friend. Fetterman rushed out and grabbed the collar of the man's shirt, helping to move him toward the redoubt.

Gerber covered them and then retreated slowly. Firing along the line became sporadic. The strikers still held the south and west walls, but the order had gone out for them to abandon those positions, too.

As the last of the men entered the redoubt, a group of strikers started throwing up a barricade of anything they could find. The pushed fifty-five-gallon drums into the entrance, rolled a jeep in and began tossing sandbags in to build a makeshift wall.

Gerber found Fetterman. "Tony, you watch them. Have them straighten it up so we don't provide Charlie with an easy climb."

"Got it, Captain."

Gerber turned and ran toward the far end of the redoubt. He passed the dispensary, which was little more than smoking rubble, then the team house, which was totally ruined. There was a command bunker built into the side of the redoubt. A tunnel led outside, near where the remains of the fire control tower lay, but Gerber knew it had collapsed. He found Fulton crouched there, a PRC-25 set up on top of the bunker, giving the antenna a little extra height.

"How're we doing?" asked Gerber.

"Not good. I've ordered the strikers on the west wall to E and E. Can't get them in here, and it seems their only hope is to escape."

"Then we've lost the west wall, too."

Fulton shook his head. "Hell, we've lost the whole outer perimeter."

"What's our status now?"

Fulton laughed. "Well, the Mike Force is still on the ground at Moc Hoa. Seems the rain has the choppers grounded. Air Force can't penetrate the clouds, and most of the artillery around here is involved in counter-battery duels. Charlie is dropping mortars on everything within range of us."

"Then we're on our own," said Gerber grimly.

"That's about the size of it."

"What about casualties?"

"Christ, I don't know. I've lost my junior commo sergeant, Hampton. Took a round in the head. Timmons is in here somewhere, and our doc is working like three people to patch up the wounded."

"Okay, Roger," said Gerber. "Let me ask you a couple of questions. One, can we get out of here?"

"There are plans for our E and E, but they assumed we'd have at least one clear way out. Right now that doesn't exist."

"Two," said Gerber. "Have you got the ammo to hold on in here?"

"All our spare ammo is in here now. But the way we're burning through it, I doubt it'll last the night. I've mined the ammo bunkers outside the redoubt, and when Charlie advances on them, we're going to blow them."

Gerber wiped a hand over his face. It was wet with sweat and the mist that was hanging over the camp. He peeled back the camouflage band on his watch, surprised that it was now one in the morning.

"I'd suggest you get on the horn and try to get a resupply chopper in here."

"He'll never make it. No place to land. And now, after the Medevac was shot down, I don't want to risk it."

"I was thinking he could buzz by and shove the ammo out the door."

Fulton shook his head. "Shit, Captain. It's not going to work. They make a concentrated effort and they're going to be able to push us out of here easily. It's over."

"It's not over until we're all dead," said Gerber. "Look, can you get the Air Force boys in here? On station?"

"I suppose we could get someone overhead."

"Then we could put some shit right on Charlie. We could guide them and let them drop on our order without them seeing the ground targets. Keep it away from the camp, out near their staging areas. We might get lucky, maybe take some heat off us."

"Yeah," said Fulton. "Okay. I'll try to get all that arranged."

"And try to get the artillery to give us fire support again. That antimortar isn't worth a shit, and we could use the illumination when the assault starts, if nothing else."

"Okay. What are you going to be doing?"

"I'm going to find Sergeant Fetterman and stick close to him. He's just nasty enough to get us all out of here alive. He knows the score."

Fulton reached out and touched Gerber's shoulder. "Glad you're here, Captain."

"Thanks. Wish I could say the same, but I really wish I was in Saigon drinking beer and chasing women."

"I heard that." Fulton was quiet for a moment and then said, "Good luck."

Gerber knew he was going to need it.

9

MIKE FORCE
DEPLOYMENT AREA
MOC HOA SPECIAL
FORCES CAMP

Santini walked into the Mike Force area and was surprised by the rows of trucks, trucks he hadn't expected to find on the base. Granted, there weren't enough of them to deploy the entire Mike Force, but there were enough to move a couple of strike companies. And, to his increased surprise, the strike companies were already loaded. Many of the Vietnamese were smoking cigarettes, the tips glowing in the dark, marking them. Santini couldn't see the men holding them.

Major Winger approached from the rear and touched Santini on the shoulder. "I make it about a hundred miles to Fulton's camp. With choppers we could be there in half an hour, forty-five minutes. In the trucks it's going to take something like three or four hours."

"Weather still the problem?"

"Exactly. This storm front's holding steady here and there are thunderstorms backed up into Cambodia. At night, in this kind of weather, the choppers can't fly. We've waited as long as we dare.''

Santini turned and looked at the officer. ''What does that mean?''

''It means, Sergeant, that Captain Fulton hasn't been able to maintain the integrity of his camp. The NVA has overrun part of the defenses. Fulton reports that most of the structures have been destroyed and the majority of his strike force is now clustered in the redoubt. We're going to move half the Mike Force out in trucks. We should reach his camp about dawn. If we can get choppers, or if the weather breaks, then the other half will be flown in. Which group do you want to go with?''

Santini nodded toward the trucks. ''I'll go with them. I don't want to be sitting around here waiting for the weather to break and then waiting for the choppers to arrive.''

''Fine. We'll be pulling out in five minutes. Do you have to coordinate with your people in Nha Trang?''

''Not now, sir. Once I'm on the scene and have an idea of the situation, I'll make a quick report when I can. Major Madden expects me to continue on to Plei Soi.''

''I'll be riding up front, in the second jeep,'' said Winger. ''You're welcome to ride along with me. You can help me with the radios.''

''Yes, sir. Thank you, sir.''

Winger turned to walk back into the main compound. Santini stepped to the jeep and dropped his rucksack and gear into the rear. He noticed that a radio had been bolted on one side. It was a large radio with a whip antenna and a tiny speaker. There was both a Fox Mike and a Uniform. With them, Winger would be able to stay in touch with practically everyone in South Vietnam.

The jeep's driver turned when he heard Santini tossing his equipment into the rear of the vehicle. "Who are you?"

"Santini. I'll be riding along. You got any spare ammo in here?"

"Couple of bandoliers of M-16."

"Think I'll grab some more. Where's the closest ammo bunker?"

The driver stared at Santini. The only thing Santini could tell about him was that he had white skin. The darkness concealed everything else.

The man lifted a hand and pointed. "Bunker over there about fifty yards."

"Thanks." Santini walked over, letting everything around him wash over him. A damp, dark night. Thunder in the distance. Thunder and artillery and bombing missions. He scanned the horizon and saw a flash of lightning.

Near the perimeter he found the ammo bunker. Before descending into it, he looked out over the approaches to Moc Hoa. The wet weather had turned the normally dry fields into small, shallow lakes, and Santini wondered if the trucks would get stuck. They might need boats.

He entered the bunker and felt along the side until his hand touched the electric lantern where the light switch would have been in a house in the World. GIs were accustomed to everything that way. Every American was used to a light switch just inside the door, so battery-powered lanterns were set on shelves built there.

Santini flicked the light on and stepped onto the wooden floor. Ammo was arranged neatly in groups so that the men, if under attack, could sort through it easily. Using his combat knife, Santini pried open a crate and pulled out a couple of cans of ammo. Before he could use the ammo, it would have to be loaded into magazines. They would need it if they got into a heavy firefight. Then he grabbed a dozen bandoliers from the peg where they hung. These were magazines already loaded with M-16 rounds.

When he finished, ne moved to the door, put the lantern on its shelf and shut it off. Then he stepped out into the night and headed back to the jeep.

Winger was sitting in the front seat when he returned. As he approached, the diesel engines of the trucks roared to life. A cloud of sparks belched into the air over one of the trucks.

"Get in," called out Winger. "We've got a long way to go and we need to make some time."

GERBER WORKED HIS WAY around the inside of the redoubt. A row of sandbags topped it, and there was a coil of concertina strung along it. The surviving strikers were gathered around, guarding the walls. Machine guns were placed at strategic points and guarded by grenadiers with M-79s. Ammo crates were stacked around the inside so that the defenders could get at it quickly and easily.

The wounded were in the center of the redoubt, protected by a row of fifty-five-gallon drums and sandbags and debris from the ruined hootches. The medics were using supplies salvaged from the fire that had gutted the dispensary.

Gerber slipped toward the entrance where Fetterman was sitting with his M-3 in his lap and two LAW rockets by his side. He was staring across the open ground toward the bunker line. Most of it was now ruined, the bunkers smoking craters.

"What's happening out there?" Gerber asked.

Fetterman looked at him. "I think they're consolidating their gains." He glanced at the low-hanging clouds and added, "With the weather the way it is, Charlie knows there's no hurry."

"Yeah," said Gerber.

There was a pop overhead, and through the clouds they could see a point of light glowing brightly. An instant later the flare burst through and the ground was illuminated. The oscillating of the flare under its parachute caused the shadows to dance and shift, making it look as if the dead were crawling toward them.

Gerber surveyed the area south of the redoubt. It seemed to him that the defense of that wall had collapsed as completely as it had on the north. Suddenly one of the bunkers exploded, throwing flaming debris over the compound. Flames shot skyward and ammunition began cooking off. Gerber realized that Fulton had made good on his promise to destroy the re-arm points if the enemy captured them.

From the south came a burst of firing. M-16s against AK. Gerber crawled forward and saw the battle shaping up on the south wall. Someone had organized the strikers around three bunkers and created a small defensive perimeter. The VC had them pinned down and were pouring a withering fire into the bunkers.

Gerber dropped back down. "Think we can liven that up some?"

Fetterman grabbed his LAWs and scrambled up the loose dirt of the redoubt. He leaned across the top and watched the developing battle. Firing from inside the redoubt increased as the strikers there tried to help those pinned down in the bunkers.

From the east side of the bunker line, a heavy machine gun opened up, putting rounds into the sandbags on the south. In the half-light from the flares and through the mist that still drifted, Fetterman saw the sandbags begin to disintegrate.

"Shit," he said. He picked up one of the LAWs and pulled the cotter pins. As he extended it, he lifted it to his shoulder, aiming at the bunker the VC now held. With one hand on the front to keep it from rising, he triggered the weapon. There was a bright flash from the back blast, and the rocket launched itself. A moment later there was an explosion as the missile slammed into the bunker. Sandbags erupted upward, outlined in the flash of fire. The concussion blew back, and Fetterman felt it hit him, but the machine gun stopped firing.

Gerber slapped his shoulder. "Well done, Master Sergeant."

Firing tapered off then, as if the VC and NVA had lost interest in the tiny perimeter. Their weapons were turned on the defenders in the redoubt. Green tracers flashed through the night. Gerber ducked, sure that he could feel the impact of the rounds on the other side of the dirt wall.

"On the east!" shouted a voice.

Gerber slipped to the ground and moved to the side of the jeep pushed into the entrance of the redoubt. Over it and the bunker line, in the open rice paddies east of the camp, he saw two full companies forming. They spread out, appearing momentarily and then dropping from sight, using the cover available to them as they rushed forward. It wasn't a surging charge, but a fire-and-maneuver attack. Shooting came in surging volleys, designed to keep the heads of the defenders down.

"Artillery support!" shouted Gerber.

"Nothing," answered Fulton, who had come up behind them quietly.

Gerber looked over his shoulder but couldn't see the other officer in the dark. "You'd better do something, because they're on their way again."

Fetterman crouched beside him. "No claymores left. Most of the bunker line's fallen." He grinned, his teeth strangely white in the yellowish-green light of the flares overhead. "Looks bad for the home team."

"Think it's time to get out?" asked Gerber.

"What do you have in mind?"

"Thought maybe it was time to call Saigon and request the chopper that was promised us. We could report that the camp should be abandoned."

"I'm with you," said Fetterman. He hesitated and then said, "It's been good working with you, Captain."

"The same, Tony."

"Here they come again," yelled a voice, and it seemed that everyone in the redoubt opened fire. There was a single, long, drawn-out crash as the men began putting out rounds. A sheet of fire seemed to roll down the sides of the redoubt and engulf the oncoming Vietcong.

The enemy returned fire. The rice paddies came alive with the strobing of the VC's weapons, looking like a hundred thousand fireflies. Again the bugles sounded, and the enemy soldiers were up on their feet, running and shouting and screaming their rage at the camp.

Gerber aimed his weapon and fired on single-shot. He kept at it as the enemy ran through gaps in the wire and reached the punji moat. He fired at the men who swarmed up the road toward the gate, which now hung on a single hinge and slowed no one. He shot at the enemy as they climbed the outer wall and leaped among the remains of the bunkers there.

The fire from the redoubt cut them down. The bodies dropped back into the punji pits or to the top of the wall. They tumbled forward, landing on the ground at the foot of the wall and among the dead defenders in their destroyed bunkers.

As that fire increased, the enemy began scrambling for cover. Slowly the targets disappeared, but the fire from the VC increased. There were more muzzle-flashes and incoming tracers. Grenades were thrown, but many of them fell short, exploding outside the redoubt. Others failed to detonate.

FULTON, WHO HAD RETURNED to the other side of the redoubt, watched the enemy storming the east wall again. The VC gained a foothold there and then stopped. Firing broke out, but it was sporadic, designed to pin down the defenders in the redoubt.

When the attack halted, far short of his position, Fulton slid down the dirt wall and crawled to the radio. It was a portable PRC-25, set up on a sandbagged bunker with the antenna sticking straight into the sky. He tried to raise one of the artillery advisories, but was told that everything in range of his camp was either firing the illumination he had requested or was firing in support of other units.

"Aircraft?" he asked.

"Be advised that Rattlesnake Two One is inbound your location."

"Say aircraft type."

"Birddog."

"Roger, Birddog. Say frequency."

"He'll come up on yours. Stand by."

A moment later the radio squawked. "Diablo Six, Diablo Six, this is Rattlesnake Two One."

"Roger, Two One. Say location."

"I should be near your camp. Do you hear my engine?"

Fulton took the handset away from his ear and strained to hear the insectlike buzz of the single-engine Cessna, but the sound of the M-16s, M-1s, AKs and rockets made it impossible.

"Negative."

"Ah, roger. I should be north of your camp. Do you have a fire arrow?"

Fulton couldn't help laughing. With the clouds down to eight or nine hundred feet and with a light drizzle, it would be impossible for anyone in the air to see the fire arrow—if he still held it, which he didn't. Charlie had overrun that portion of the camp when he had taken the north wall.

"That's a negative."

"Roger. Be advised I will fire willie pete rockets north of the camp. Please spot."

Fulton crawled up the side of the redoubt and looked over the top, but saw nothing. He reported that.

"Roger. Wait one."

Fulton slipped down so that his head was below the top of the redoubt. He listened carefully and heard the firing taper as if both sides were tired. Then through that noise cut the drone of an aircraft engine. He had been in the gun target lines south of the camp. Fulton shuddered when he realized that the pilot could have flown into one of the flares.

"You're over the camp," he shouted into the mike. "You're over the camp." He shook his head. The silly son of a bitch had been south of him when he'd fired the rockets.

"Understood. I have two fully loaded aircraft inbound. Where do you want it?"

"Wait one," said Fulton. He moved back to the top and peeked over it. Men were moving on the north side—some of them in the bunkers and some of them in the rice paddies and in the wire beyond. Staging areas and rally points seemed to be in the trees about three hundred meters to the north.

"Two One, put it on the north side of the camp about three hundred meters out."

"Roger. Do you still hear my engines?"

"Negative."

And then there was the roar of the single engine as the plane came flashing out of the night, hopping across the rice paddies and wire of the perimeter. It was so low and came so close that Fulton could see the glow from the cockpit instruments. The tiny plane grew rapidly until it seemed giant-sized, and then all the VC and NVA opened fire on it. Green tracers stabbed upward, knifing toward the little craft.

As it flew over the redoubt, it banked sharply west and began a climb that looked straight up. It disappeared into the clouds a second later, followed by hundreds of green tracers.

"Diablo Six, this is Two One."

Fulton didn't respond for a moment. He was in awe. The pilot had to be crazy. Flying through the mist that hung over the camp, dodging around the flares as they descended toward the ground, was not the act of a sane man. It had been an inspiring act. If the pilot could pull that off, Fulton was sure he could hold his camp. Too many crazy Americans were out there who would do anything to help him.

"Go, Two One."

"Roger, understand your situation. I will put rockets into the trees north of the camp."

"Roger. I will try to spot for you."

As he peered through the night, he heard the roar of jet engines far to the north. The fighters, loaded with bombs, napalm and 20 mm cannon rounds, had arrived. He glanced at the cloud cover but could see nothing above him.

There were two distant explosions in the trees north of the camp, just as the pilot had promised. Fulton saw the flashes of the explosions and the eruptions of fire and flame from the white phosphorus.

"You're on the target," said Fulton. "Hit them hard."

He ducked, waited, and when he heard the scream of the jet as it dived toward the target, he peeked again. Orange fireballs had set the jungle on fire—white-hot flashes that could melt the flesh from bones and incinerate trees. The roar from the jet faded and then came again as the second plane rolled in.

He missed the jungle, dropping his napalm into the open ground between the camp and the trees. In the flames, Fulton was sure he could see human shapes. Something burning, trailing flames and fire, ran from the inferno. It semaphored its arms as it wavered and then collapsed into a burning ball.

Explosions ripped the jungle as the first plane made a second run. Not the quiet, dull pops of mortars or the flat bangs of the rockets, but gigantic rolling thunder that threatened to kill by concussion alone.

As the second jet made another run, the jungle erupted into fire as a thousand weapons poured tracers into the sky. Lines of green streaked upward, disappearing in the clouds. But that didn't stop the jet. It dropped its load and turned, and the ground vibrated as the bombs exploded.

Cheering erupted from the redoubt. A hundred strikers, seeing the enemy die in horrible ways, cheered the pilots who had braved the night and the rain to get to them. They cheered as the enemy died.

Now cannon fire from the machine guns on the jets poured into the ground. Lines of ruby tracers fought through the green and ripped up the jungle, shredding trees, bushes and human bodies.

"Diablo Six, this is Two One."

"Go."

"I've two more aircraft inbound. You want it in the same place?"

"Negative. Put it on the east side of the camp. I say again, put it on the east side of the camp."

"Roger. Putting rockets down."

Fulton turned and looked east over the broken and burning bunkers that now belonged to the enemy, over the bodies of the men who had died in the fighting, and out into the rice paddies. He didn't know how far away the enemy staging points might be, but he wanted something dumped on the east side of the camp.

And then there were the twin explosions of the marking rockets, looking as if they were right on target. Fulton squeezed the mike button. "That's got it."

The show was repeated there. Napalm first and then high explosive. Fulton wondered if it shouldn't be the other way. High explosives to drive the enemy from hiding, then napalm to burn the evidence. Not that he cared now, because the air assault had stopped the enemy. They were burning through their ammo, firing into the sky.

Around him, his men were shooting, too, aiming at the muzzle-flashes of the enemy weapons, trying to kill them while their attention was on the planes overhead.

"Diablo Six, I will remain on station for another hour. No more air strikes will be going on for a while. Weather has deteriorated in Saigon."

"Roger," said Fulton. He knew it meant the Air Force was having trouble getting fighters up into the weather. He wasn't sure the risk to the pilots was worth the results, although it did divert Charlie's attention and improved the morale of his own men.

Then, almost as if to prove he hadn't forgotten about the men in the redoubt, Charlie began lobbing mortar rounds again. It was a tricky operation because Charlie had his own men scattered throughout the camp and a short or long round could fall among his own troops.

A bright flash came from the east side of the redoubt as Fetterman fired the last of his LAW rockets. There was a fiery explosion in the field as the missile slammed into a rice paddy dike, but that didn't slow the enemy mortars.

Fulton glanced across the redoubt but couldn't see Fetterman. He smiled to himself, sure that Fetterman would be thinking of ways to harass the enemy as they came storming over the walls of the redoubt.

He hoped that would be enough to keep the enemy outside the camp. Fetterman and the men grouped around him had to be enough. The relief column, according to the CO at Moc Hoa, had left the camp. If they could hold until it arrived, two hours at the most, then they could all get out of it alive.

10

EN ROUTE TO CAMP A-337

Santini was fascinated by the movement of the convoy through the night. They stayed on the paved roads leading out of Moc Hoa, first to the east and slightly to the south, and then back to the north. In areas where there were forests of jungle, the trees had been cut back so that they were no closer than a hundred meters to the edge of the road. At the head of the convoy and at the rear were MP jeeps, each mounted with an M-60 machine gun manned by an MP. Other jeeps were scattered throughout the convoy, and several of the trucks were armed with M-60s. The one in the center had a Browning M-2 .50-caliber machine gun. Men stood behind each of those weapons, ready for trouble. Others were on guard, searching the dark rainy night for the enemy.

Winger turned in his seat. "We're going to stop at B-32, that is, at Tay Ninh West, for a quick update before continuing. I don't like this at all."

"Yes, sir," said Santini.

"I'd like to get some choppers up to survey the road in front of us. This is perfect for Charlie. A perfect opportunity for an ambush."

The words were barely out of his mouth when an explosion ripped through the night. The flash of light and fire destroyed the lead jeep. The blast lifted the vehicle's front end and then dropped it. The driver flipped out, landing on the road, the rain pelting on his back. He didn't move.

The trees on the right side of the convoy began flashing as the NVA platoon opened fire. The rounds, from AKs and RPDs, ripped into the trucks, slamming into the tires and into the men sitting in the backs of the trucks. There was shouting, screaming, crying. A few men shot back, and the heavy machine gun opened up, chugging momentarily and then falling silent as the man behind it was killed.

Santini snatched his weapon and vaulted from the jeep. He rolled to the wet tarmac and pointed his rifle at the enemy position, but didn't fire. He watched the flashing in the tree line as the VC poured a devastating fusillade into the convoy.

Winger crawled across the driver's seat and dropped to the ground. He worked his way around so that he was leaning against the rear tire and was able to look at Santini.

"This was what I was afraid of. I knew they'd hit us. I knew it."

"Yeah," said Santini.

Winger stood up and grabbed the microphone on the radios and squeezed it.

Grenades began to explode among the trucks. Dull, quiet pops flashed like firecrackers in tin cans. Shrapnel rattled against the metal of the trucks, punched through the canvas and splintered the wood on the sides.

Santini rolled to his right and saw one of the Special Forces sergeants on his feet running along the sides of the trucks. He was shouting at the Vietnamese, telling them to open fire. He kicked at them, grabbed some and threw them to the ground, ordering them to shoot into the jungle. He stopped once, burned through a whole magazine, then started moving again.

Slowly the Vietnamese began to return fire. M-79s lobbed grenades at the trees. There were explosions at the edge of the jungle. The .50 caliber began to hammer again, the huge tracers punching into the enemy lines.

Santini crawled to the first truck in the convoy. He lay next to the tire and aimed into the winking muzzle-flashes that marked the enemy's weapons. He squeezed off a couple of rounds, heard one snap into the tire near his head and ducked. The tire began to hiss as the air escaped.

Now the firing was a continual roar, and the air thick with ruby tracers. Santini wiped the rain from his face and emptied his magazine. He rolled to his left, pulled another magazine from his bandolier and slammed it home.

At the far end of the convoy, one of the SF NCOs was trying to organize an assault force. It was obvious he wanted to flank the enemy. Santini got to his feet and moved to the rear where the road sloped away from the center. He ran through the ditch, splashing the water that had gathered there. As he reached the rear of the convoy, he slipped to one knee and waited.

Firing from the jungle had slowed. Santini got up and ran to the truck. He heard the American say, "We spread out and run for the trees. We stop short."

At that moment there was a shuttering sound and then an eruption inside the tree line. Within seconds there was another and another, until the artillery began to explode throughout the trees. Flashes of orange fire from the trucks increased, then tapered off. A ragged cheer rose from the side of the road.

As that died there were calls for medics. Men were shouting at one another, searching for friends. Then there were more explosions from the trees as another volley found its range.

Santini turned and ran back to the front. He found Winger sitting on the ground, his back to the rear tire of the jeep, handset jammed against his ear. He was shouting over the radio, calling in the artillery.

Santini dropped next to him and waited. Winger moved the handset from his ear and said, "That's it."

"Meaning?"

"We stay here. Can't move until first light."

Santini wanted to protest, but knew that Winger was right. They had taken casualties and they had sustained damage. Now the fire support bases around them knew where they were and could be called on to lend artillery fire.

Winger rubbed a hand over his face and looked at Santini. "Look, I want to get up there as badly as you do, but right now there's nothing I can do. We move and run into another ambush, everyone's dead. We have to stay here."

"I understand, sir. I just hope those boys can hold out."

Winger tossed the handset into the jeep. He shook his head. "I was afraid of this. I didn't want to travel at night without scouts. Damn rain. Fucking damn rain."

"Yes, sir," said Santini.

"Look, I want you to find out the status of the trucks. Get parties organized to repair them. Push those too heavily damaged out of the way. At dawn, as soon as we can get the aircraft in here, we take off. What do the casualties look like? We get hurt?"

"No more than five or six dead and about twice that wounded. If we could get a Medevac in here, that would take care of the problem with the wounded."

Winger looked up at the sky, but could see nothing other than the black undersides of the cloud cover. There was no sign of the stars or moon, or the rain that had been falling off and on. He grabbed the handset from the back seat of the jeep and keyed the mike. "Crusader Ops, this is Epsilon Six."

"Go, Six."

"Roger. We need a Medevac in here."

There was a pause and then a quiet voice said, "Say condition of the wounded."

Winger looked at Santini who said, "Two are critical, one is serious and the rest are minor and could become serious if they don't get out of here."

Winger repeated the message.

"Roger. Wait one."

"What's the deal?" Winger asked Santini.

"I don't know, Major."

The radio crackled to life. "Are you in contact?"

"Negative. LZ is secure and cold."

"Roger. Say location."

Winger yanked a map from his pocket and opened it, reading the grid coordinates. He didn't want to give them in the clear, even though it was apparent that his position had been compromised by the ambush. Instead, he told Crusader Operations that the coordinates were down from Benny's age. That told the men in Crusader Ops that they had to subtract thirty-nine from every number given to them.

"Roger. Aircraft will be inbound your location in one five minutes."

"Roger," said Winger.

Santini looked at his watch. There were still three hours of darkness, and the rain had begun to fall again. He didn't think they were going to make it in time.

FROM OVERHEAD CAME THE ROAR of fighters, searching the clouds for a break. There was the pop of flares as the artillery kept the illumination above them. Gerber lay on the damp earth of the redoubt, watching for the enemy. Around him was the rattle of small arms as the VC and NVA tried to overwhelm the remaining pockets of resistance.

Next to him the strikers fired in support of their friends barricaded in bunkers around the perimeter. Machine gun fire ripped through the night. Gerber spotted one of the machine gun nests: a heavy weapon, partially concealed by the ruins of a bunker and the debris scattered in the fighting. Smoke pouring from the eastern end of the line obscured the weapon, but Gerber could see the muzzle-flashes and the line of green tracers pouring from it.

"Tony," he called out, "you got another of those LAWs?"

"See what I can do, Captain."

As Fetterman turned to run back across the interior of the redoubt, Gerber began pumping rounds into the smoke and mist that hid the enemy. At first he fired single-shot, wishing he had a shotgun with the range to scatter pellets into the smoke. Then he switched to full-auto and sprayed the area, but the enemy machine gun kept chugging, blasting away at the strikers on the south wall, destroying their protection and killing some of them.

Fetterman returned moments later. "Couldn't find a LAW, but I located an M-79." He dropped a bandolier next to Gerber and crawled upward, careful to keep his head below the lip of the embankment. He broke open the weapon. "What do you think?"

"You got any WP?"

"Four or five rounds. Got some HE and canister rounds."

"Okay," said Gerber. "Use two WP to start. I'll mark with tracers."

Fetterman loaded his weapon, flipped up the sight and adjusted it. Then he decided it wouldn't be of any use. He snapped it down, risked a quick peek at the target and said, "Whenever you're ready."

Gerber looked over the top and switched magazines so that the one he had was loaded only with tracers. He nodded and then popped up, firing rapidly.

Beside him, Fetterman aimed and fired, dropping before the round impacted.

Gerber saw the explosion: a feathery white-hot cloud that didn't slow the firing of the enemy machine gun, its glowing, emerald tracers tearing into the south side of the camp.

"Missed. To the west," said Gerber. "Maybe twenty yards. Maybe less."

He slipped down and looked at the master sergeant. "I'll mark again and try to do better."

As he popped up, firing, Fetterman did the same. He triggered the M-79 and ducked again. Gerber saw the round detonate into the fiery mountain of white. The enemy machine gun stopped shooting. There was a secondary explosion and then a fireworks display as the ammo began cooking off, the green tracers tumbling into the night.

"That got it," shouted Gerber.

Fetterman looked up at him, the opened M-79 cradled in his hands. "Knew we'd do it."

"For now, anyway," said Gerber.

MINH SLOWLY BECAME AWARE of his surroundings. He could smell the wet dirt near his nose and feel a heaviness on his legs. His face was pushed into the mud, with his neck at an uncomfortable angle. As he shifted around slightly, he saw that he was partially trapped under the remains of the fire control tower and the sandbags that had been on it. There was an ache in his legs and his back, and when he opened his eyes he could see almost nothing except a tiny patch of mud and a small portion of the redoubt.

He could still hear firing around him. No longer was it the concentrated volleys that suggested the enemy was attacking in force. It was sporadic and scattered, and Minh wondered if his strikers still held the camp, or if the enemy had finally managed to overrun it.

He pulled a hand down under his shoulder and tried to free himself. Although he strained, he couldn't move his legs. He rolled to the right and felt pain shoot along his thighs and into his back. Sweat beaded his forehead, but he ignored it and the pain.

Shifting carefully, he managed to grab the top of a sandbag and yank it free. He pushed another away and felt the stack across him move. Fearing that the whole pile of rubble was going to shift and crush him, he sucked in his breath, holding it for a moment. Then he realized everything was going to hold. Noticing a looseness near his trapped foot, he jerked on it and felt it pop free.

For a moment he lay quietly, breathing hard and listening to the shooting around him. He twisted his head from side to side but couldn't see any living VC or NVA. There were bodies visible in the half-light from the flares and through the mist that covered the camp.

Certain that no one was watching, Minh sat up and pulled at his trapped leg. It moved but scraped on something, which dug into his leg sharply, and he felt blood begin to flow. Cursing quietly under his breath, he forced his foot deeper into the rubble and then leaned forward. Slowly he dug his way out until the pressure on his trapped limb lifted and he could free it without further injury. When it came loose, he leaned back against the twisted wreckage of the fire control tower and tried to relax.

Finally he rolled away from the pile of sandbags and rubble. He stretched out next to the tower and tried to assess the situation. The northern bunker line was a smoking ruin. The bodies of the dead strikers lay scattered around it. Equipment lay everywhere, bent and broken, or destroyed as the Americans and strikers had abandoned the bunker line. Movement in the shadows suggested that the Vietcong and NVA had captured all the positions but that they weren't making an attempt to hold them.

A dead VC lay near him. Minh reached out and snagged the collar of the enemy's shirt and pulled him closer. The man had a wound in his face that exposed his teeth, making it seem as if he were grinning in death. A canvas pouch on his chest held extra banana clips for an AK-47. He wore a pistol belt with a canteen that looked American.

Minh stripped everything from the body and donned
the equipment himself. He shed his American-made
boots and stole the dead man's sandals. Then, crawling
from the protection of the tower, he grabbed an AK-47.
Although it was wet from the rain and mist, he wasn't
worried about it blowing up if he fired it. The barrel was
clear of mud. He ejected one live round to make sure a
fresh one was chambered and then checked the magazine. It, too, was clear of mud, and it seemed to be fully
loaded.

Now, armed and disguised, Minh crouched and ran
toward the bunker line. He ignored the pain, more worried that his own soldiers, still holding the redoubt as far
as he could tell, would shoot him. He didn't try to gain
access, figuring that one side or the other would kill him.
He had done enough for one night, and it was time to get
out. If he succeeded in that, he might find some other
strikers, if any of them had gotten out, and organize
some kind of defense until help arrived in the morning.

He dropped to the mud near a couple of bodies, but
didn't check them. He watched the bunker line, and
when he saw that the VC and NVA were avoiding one of
the bunkers, he ran to it, falling into the mud just behind it. Again he hesitated, listening to the small-arms
fire around him, much of it to the south, near the bunker
line there, or on the east, directed toward the redoubt.

He scrambled over the pile of torn and smoking sandbags and found himself inside the bunker that looked
more like a crater now. The remains of two strikers were
there, both killed by the satchel charge that had ripped
the bunker apart. The bodies were so mutilated that
Minh couldn't tell who they had been. It was hard even
identifying the remains as human beings. The .30-

caliber machine gun was little more than a twisted lump of metal and splintered wood.

Without examining the scene too closely, Minh slipped over the front of the bunker and found himself outside the camp. He worked his way down the berm to the punji moat, but there was no way to cross it where he was. He moved along, keeping to the dancing shadows caused by the swinging of the parachute flares until he came to a narrow path through the punji moat that wouldn't be obvious to an attacking enemy, but was there in case the defenders had to get out.

Minh dived to the ground there and rested. He realized his leg was hurting badly and wondered if he had managed to break it. There was a sharp pain in his side each time he breathed, and he was certain a rib or two had been fractured. And to make everything worse, if possible, he was thirsty and his breath rasped in his throat. Although he knew it was a reaction to the situation, it made the desire for water no less intense. But slaking his thirst was something that would have to wait.

Feeling as rested as possible, he crawled forward slowly, hoping that any of the enemy who saw him now would think he was a wounded VC soldier trying to reach medical aid. He wormed his way through the punji moat, avoiding the razor-sharp bamboo stakes. When he came to the end of it, he crawled up the berm and rolled out onto the killing field of wire that surrounded the camp.

Just as he reached it, the last of the flares burned itself out, and there was a momentary blackness around the camp. It was an opportunity that was too good to pass up. Minh leaped to his feet and ran as fast as his wounded leg allowed him. He jogged through the wire, reaching the last strand, then moved into the rice paddies beyond, before he heard the telltale pop above the camp. Knowing that a flare would burn through the cloud cover quickly, he fell behind a low rice paddy dike and waited.

When the camp was again bathed in the eerie, flickering light of the flare, he saw the damage. Little of the camp remained. All the buildings were gone. The bunker line was little more than a cratered line that smoked heavily. Fires still burned, but most of them were small, the rain and mist holding them down or extinguishing them.

Minh was overwhelmed by the sight. It was worse than the attack on Camp A-555 after the VC-reinforced regiment had tried to overrun it.

He wished he had an M-16 in his hands as he waited for the enemy to attack. It was obvious that someone still held the redoubt because of the firing around it. But there was no way for him to get to it, and anyway, someone was bound to shoot him long before he could reach its safety.

The only intelligent thing for him to do was try to get to the jungle. Once there, he could hide until the American rescue column arrived to retake the camp. He knew a column would be sent; they always sent one.

But intelligence couldn't smother the feeling in the pit of his stomach. He should be inside the camp waiting for the final assault to come. He shouldn't be outside, safe from the enemy. Or as safe as anyone could be with a regiment of the enemy nearby. It wasn't right that he'd gotten out.

And to make it worse, Minh knew that by lying low, he would be able to survive until the rescue party came. There was nothing more he could do. The irony was that if he stayed where he was and was rescued, he would be treated as a hero, although all he had done was run. But then, there was no way for him to get back into the camp without sacrificing himself for no reason. He had to stay where he was.

Realizing the flares over the camp were too far away to expose him, Minh began crawling toward the jungle. He ignored the desire to return to the camp. If he moved slowly, he knew he wouldn't be spotted.

When he reached the edge of the jungle, he looked back at the remains of Camp A-337. The surviving defenders were still fighting; he could see the ruby tracers from their weapons. The Vietnamese captain got to his feet and held on to the smooth trunk of a teak tree. He blinked rapidly, trying to stop the tears filling his eyes. Silently he said, "Good luck, chaps."

GERBER HAD STOPPED firing at the enemy. He was watching the area around the redoubt, waiting for the attack he knew had to come, but he hadn't seen an enemy soldier in nearly a quarter of an hour.

He heard a noise behind him and then heard Fulton say, "Captain Gerber, I'd like to talk to you and Sergeant Fetterman for a moment."

Gerber glanced at the eastern bunker line but saw no evidence that the enemy was going to attack soon. The firing had tapered off to potshots taken by soldiers on either side. Gerber slid down. "What do you need?"

"Come with me."

The three of them moved across the redoubt and around the makeshift dispensary and the remains of the team house. They came to Timmons, who was crouched near the ruins of a bunker, the PRC-25 still set up high so that the antenna would be above the tops of the embankment.

As they approached, he shook his head. "Nothing more on the radio, sir."

They crouched in the dark and Fulton said, "We've lost radio contact with everyone. I don't know where half my team is, and Captain Minh has been killed."

Fetterman interrupted. "You sure Minh is dead?"

"He was in the fire control tower when it was knocked down, and no one has seen him since," said Timmons.

"Jesus," said Gerber. "Minh was a good one. Damn. You sure he's dead?"

Timmons snapped, "If you came around the fire control tower, you must have seen the body."

Gerber thought about the legs that had been sticking out from under a pile of sandbags and wondered if that had been Minh. There was no time to worry about it now. He would drink a beer in Minh's honor, if he managed to survive the night.

Fulton began again, saying, "You know as much about this as the rest of us. I know there are pockets of resistance, but I figure the VC are going to take them out one by one until only we remain. Then they'll deal with us."

"No communications with them?" asked Gerber.

"None. Radios are all out. Field phones are worthless. All the lines have been cut. We're on our own in here."

Gerber looked at the men on the walls of the redoubt. Each of them was watching the ground outside. Each held a weapon and a few were firing. At the base of the wall were the bodies of the men killed, lying where they had fallen. Equipment, weapons and rubble were strewn everywhere. Gerber made a quick count. There were seventy-five men there.

To his left, to the east, was the makeshift dispensary. Fifty-five-gallon drums, short walls of sandbags and crates that had held ammo protected it. One American medic and two Vietnamese were working, rushing from man to man, using the little medicine and the few bandages that remained.

"Is there a way out of here?" asked Gerber.

"The best we can hope for is to use the tunnel that leads to the command post, although some of it's exposed now. I think part of it collapsed, but we should be able to dig our way out. That at least gets us out of the redoubt."

"Any provisions once we reach there?" asked Fetterman.

Fulton looked at the master sergeant. "We'd have to get to the bunker line. There are paths through the punji moats and the wires that only I, the team and Captain Minh know about. If we can get to that point, we can get out of the camp."

Gerber nodded. "Okay. So what do we do now?"

"I make it about another two hours or so until dawn. If we can hold on until then, I believe we'll get reinforcements in from Moc Hoa. Last radio message I had from Moc Hoa said that two companies were en route. The reinforcements will probably come in with the light."

Gerber looked at his watch, surprised again by the passage of time. First it had been so slow and now it seemed to be racing by, although it was still a couple of hours before the sun would come up. "Okay, Captain," said Gerber. "I think we can hold out until then."

"Yeah, I do, too. But . . ." He hesitated, looking from one blackened face to the next, aware of the sounds around them. He then checked the redoubt and the sky overhead. Even though they hadn't been in contact with the fire support bases, the artillery men kept the flares coming. If they had been overrun, the flares wouldn't hurt, and if they hadn't, the light could make all the difference. The flares would continue until the sun came up the next morning.

"Gentlemen," said Fulton. "I think the next two or three hours are going to be critical. If the defense caves in, you need to get back here as quickly as possible so that we can E and E."

"Are there any wounded Americans inside the redoubt?" asked Fetterman.

"No, just the one medic and Timmons here."

"I saw Lopez get it," said Timmons. "He tried to retake one of the bunkers. The whole thing blew up as he rushed it. I don't think he knew what hit him."

"Shit," said Fulton. "Goddamn it anyway."

"The four of us need to take care of one another if we're going to get out of this. None of us leaves until we can all get out," said Gerber.

"Right," said Timmons.

"Captain, you and Sergeant Fetterman can punch out whenever you please. Timmons and I will make sure we get Carlson out, and we'll get back to look for the rest of the team. I've got to determine what happened to them."

"We're all in this together, Captain," said Gerber. "We have to stick together."

Fulton smiled then. "Yeah. Thanks. Now I suggest we get back to our posts and wait for the assault. It's got to come anytime now. Charlie can't wait for ever." He was quiet for an instant and then added hastily, "Listen, it's been good to know you."

11

SPECIAL FORCES CAMP
A-337

The rains came again, and so did the VC. There was a crack of thunder and a boom of artillery, and the ground around Gerber and Fetterman flashed and exploded. The rain sizzled around them as the enemy opened fire, their muzzle-flashes lost in the lightning. The roar of the weapons combined with the weather to drown out the shouting and screaming as the VC made their final attack on the Special Forces camp at Plei Soi.

Gerber crouched below the lip of the redoubt, the rain soaking through his uniform and drumming on his helmet. The flares kept the landscape lighted, but the rain made it difficult to see the attacking enemy.

For an instant Gerber wished the assault wouldn't come. He just wanted to rest and relax. He didn't want to deal with the constant pressure of trying to stay alive, or of keeping everyone else alive. He wanted to be back in the swamps of North Carolina, training other soldiers. It would be raining and miserable there, but not deadly.

And then it was too late for wishful thinking because the Vietcong and the NVA were charging across the debris-littered, body-strewn thirty meters that separated the redoubt from the bunker line. Gerber popped up and looked at the ghostly gray shapes of the enemy, partially hidden by the curtain of rain. He began to fire, slowly at first, as if he had to warm up to the task.

Finally, with the enemy swarming at them and the bullets almost matching the raindrops in intensity in the air, Gerber flipped the selector to full-auto and began spraying the onrushing attackers. He burned through his magazine, dropped it clear and jammed another one home.

The Vietcong were closer now, dodging around the debris, the oil drums, the ammo crates, the ruined equipment and the dead. But the attack didn't falter as the firing increased and many VC died.

They reached the earthwork embankment and began to scramble toward the top. Those in the rear, still near the ruined bunkers, fired rapidly, trying to pin down the defenders. The first few who gained the top of the redoubt were shot or bayoneted. Some of the bodies fell inside the wall, but the majority remained outside.

Gerber grabbed the shirt of a VC soldier, leaned a hip into the man and flipped him to the ground. He shot the assailant, then turned back to the attacking force.

The captain triggered his weapon again. Enemy soldiers toppled out of the way, revealing even more of them. They leaped over the dead and wounded and swarmed up the embankment. Gerber emptied his weapon, but there wasn't time to reload. He tossed the M-16 away, grabbed the nearest VC soldier and mashed a hand into his throat. As the man began to collapse, Gerber grabbed the barrel of the AK-47 and jerked it from the soldier's hand. The American swung the weapon like a baseball bat, slamming the wooden stock into the side of the enemy's head. Over the sound of the rain and the shooting, Gerber swore he could hear the crack of bone as the soldier died.

The Special Forces captain used the bayonet then. He thrust at a VC who stood on the top of the redoubt and felt the blade penetrate the soft flesh of the man's belly. The VC's face changed from a look of rage to one of surprise and pain. He dropped his weapon and clutched at his stomach as Gerber ripped the bayonet free. As he toppled to his side, drawing his knees up and shrieking, Gerber spun to face another VC. He fired the AK, stitching his adversary from crotch to throat.

FETTERMAN HAD SLOWLY RETREATED when the enemy had come over the top of the redoubt. Now he fired as fast as he could with his M-3, giving ground slowly as more of the enemy appeared.

He moved back until he was near the makeshift dispensary, crouching behind a fifty-five-gallon drum. He watched the hand-to-hand fight, and when one of the enemy broke through, Fetterman leaped to meet him. Sidestepping the soldier, the master sergeant turned and clipped the man in the neck as he went by. The soldier was dead before he hit the ground.

When he looked at the top of the redoubt, he knew they wouldn't be able to hold it. There were too few defenders. The only sensible thing was to try to escape and evade until they could get back to American lines.

Fetterman rushed forward to where Gerber was fighting. As a VC came at the captain from his blind side, Fetterman stepped in the way, kicking at the enemy. The man dropped and Fetterman shot him.

"Captain. It's time to get out!" the master sergeant yelled.

Gerber turned and nodded. "Lead on."

Fetterman retreated again to the dispensary where the Special Forces medic was working over the wounded.

Gerber shouted at him. "We've lost it. We can't hold this place. Let's get out."

"No, sir," said the man. "Can't move the wounded."

Gerber moved closer to the medic. He was a short, thin man with a white face that looked distraught in the harsh light of the flares. His uniform was soaked and torn, and Gerber couldn't help but admire the man's resolve, even though the wounded were all Vietnamese and would probably be shot the moment the VC captured them.

"It's an order," said Gerber, hoping he could save the young medic.

He understood immediately. "I appreciate it, Captain, but I'll have to refuse."

Gerber nodded. "Good luck, then."

Fetterman motioned to the captain that it was time to move, then started running across the redoubt to the trench that would get them out of there. Gerber followed. Fetterman dived into the trench, turned and opened fire again. He shot two men who were scrambling down the inside of the redoubt embankment, each carrying AK-47s. They fell, tumbling to the bottom where they lay still.

"Looks bad, Captain."

"Worst I've seen," said Gerber. He realized that he still carried the AK-47, but it was now empty. He tossed it to the side, then looked around until he found an M-16. He snatched it off the muddy ground and pulled out the magazine. On inspection, the barrel seemed to be clear. He reloaded and jacked a round in the chamber.

The defense on the redoubt began to collapse. The strikers, realizing they were about to be overrun by the enemy, either abandoned their positions, surrendered or died. The shooting became sporadic, coming in bursts and then in single shots as the VC attempted to mop up the resistance.

Fetterman eased around Gerber and made his way along the trench until he was near the wall of the redoubt. He crouched there and peered into the darkness, but couldn't tell whether or not the tunnel was intact. Looking up, he saw a VC running toward him, his head down. Fetterman aimed and fired, the round driving into the top of the man's head. He took two more staggering steps and then dropped into the mud.

As they watched helplessly, the dispensary was overrun. The VC moved among the wounded, shooting and bayoneting them. The medic had thrown away his medical kit and had grabbed an M-16. He was hiding behind a drum, shooting the enemy as fast as he could.

An NVA soldier appeared on the redoubt behind the medic and took aim at the SF soldier's back. Fetterman didn't hesitate. He dropped the NVA with a well-placed shot.

The medic got to his feet and ran across the compound. Bullets snapped at his heels, digging at the mud and splashing the standing water, but miraculously, none hit him. When he was close to the trench, he launched himself into a belly flop, hit the bottom hard and lay still.

Fetterman crouched near the medic. Over the sounds of the battle the master sergeant could hear him rasping for breath. He grabbed the man's shoulder. "You hit?"

The medic turned a smiling face to Fetterman. "Knocked the wind out."

The fighting tapered off then, as if the assault had run out of steam. The enemy now held the walls of the redoubt and the ruins of most of the buildings on the inside. They had overrun the gate and the team house. There was sniping, as the few survivors fought it out with the VC and NVA, but there were no assaults. The enemy was content to toss grenades and shout propaganda phrases at the survivors.

As Fetterman watched, a shape dragged itself toward them. The master sergeant covered it, suspecting a trick, but held his fire. He wanted to be sure of his target. A moment later he recognized Sergeant Timmons.

"You hit?" Fetterman rasped at him.

Timmons shook his head. He glanced over his shoulder and saw that no one was near him. He leaped up, sprinted the few feet that separated him from the trench, and dived into it, popping up again immediately.

"Where's Fulton?" asked Gerber.

Timmons shrugged. "I lost sight of him."

Gerber dropped and shook his head. "Damn. Wish he was here. Anyone else out there?"

"Sergeant Jones was hit," said Timmons. "I couldn't get to him. I tried, but I couldn't make it."

"What do you think, Tony?"

Fetterman shook his head. "I think we've bought it this time."

Gerber looked at his watch. "I make it another hour to dawn." He wiped the rain from his face and then stood to survey the inside of the redoubt. It was obvious that there weren't many of the strikers left alive.

"What's the plan, Captain?" Fetterman asked.

"I think we should wait until the last minute and then try to get out. That tunnel open, Tony?"

"I'll check it."

"Hurry up. I don't think we've got long."

SANTINI CROUCHED NEAR the rear tire of the command jeep and listened to the static of the radio as it popped and buzzed. The rain had finally stopped, leaving them all wet and cold. Winger was kneeling on the tarmac, looking across the driver's seat toward the jungle. He held his weapon ready, but there had been no firing since the ambush.

Santini moved toward Winger. "What now?"

"Cloud cover is lifting and the choppers have left Tay Ninh. Should be here in ten, fifteen minutes. We'll take half the force in the choppers to Camp A-337. The rest will stay here and get the trucks ready to return to Moc Hoa."

"Choppers can get in here?"

"As soon as it's light there won't be a problem." Winger pointed to the east. "Besides, the sun's beginning to come up. Just a few minutes more."

Santini turned. He could see the trees now, a more defined area than the black smudge they had been during the night. Men appeared at the edge of the forest, moving slowly across the open field. Santini recognized them as strikers who had gone into the trees to check out the damage inflicted by the artillery.

As the men approached, the strikers broke off, heading toward the rear of the stalled convoy. The Special Forces sergeant came toward the jeep and sat down on the wet tarmac, his back against the front tire.

"Didn't find much," he said. "Couple of damaged weapons and two bodies. We could make another sweep at dawn, but I doubt we'd find much. If there were blood trails to follow, I imagine the rain will have washed much of it away."

"No matter," said Winger. "I was only interested in making sure the enemy had pulled out."

"Yes, sir. I couldn't find any evidence that Charlie was still there. I think he pulled out almost as soon as he opened fire."

In the distance they heard the popping of rotor blades. The radio crackled to life, and the lead pilot told Winger they were inbound.

Winger plucked the mike off the back of the jeep. "Crusader One Two, roger."

"We're going to orbit for ten minutes until it gets a little lighter and then we'll land. Will you throw smoke?" asked the lead pilot.

"Roger. Give us the word."

"Roger."

Winger tossed the mike into the jeep and sat down again. He took a deep breath. "Okay. I want fifty men split into five loads and I want them moved out into the field away from the trucks."

"Yes, sir," said Santini. "I'll get on it."

He got up and hurried to the rear. He found one of the Vietnamese lieutenants and passed the instructions on to him. He watched the lieutenant find a sergeant, and in a minute there were grumbling men moving from the relative comfort of the trucks and out into the open fields. Santini joined them, stepping over the narrow ditch and onto a muddy ridge. He dropped from it into knee-deep water and splashed his way out. He joined a group of Vietnamese standing around.

Overhead was the sound of the choppers. They circled like birds looking for a way to get to the ground. Santini glanced at the trucks and noticed they were now easily visible. A gray mist wrapped the ground, but the light was improving and he could see the trucks and the men around them.

At the command jeep, Winger was again on the radio. Then he put a hand to his mouth and yelled, "Pop a smoke!"

Santini looked at the Vietnamese lieutenant and then shrugged. He grabbed the single smoke grenade he had, pulled the pin and tossed it out. It disappeared with a splash, but the smoke began to billow. A moment later, to the south, Santini saw the helicopters coming at them. They were all low, their rotors in the clouds, but they were coming straight in. The roar from their engines and the popping of the blades seemed to deflect off the clouds and the ground so that the noise built until it threatened to deafen everyone.

The helicopters came in slowly, the formation vibrating as the choppers bounced and danced, trying to maintain their positions. Then they hovered forward, their rotor wash whipping at the ground and the men. Instinctively Santini placed his hand on his helmet, although the rotor wash couldn't budge it.

As the lead chopper came even with them, it stopped. And though it sank slowly until the skids were touching the surface of the water, it didn't set down. Santini splashed to it and lifted himself up onto the skid. The chopper rocked with the sudden addition of his weight.

A hand shot out and grabbed him, dragging him into the helicopter. He scrambled onto the troop seat, then turned to help one of the Vietnamese climb aboard. Both the crew chief and the door gunner were doing the same thing. In seconds they were loaded.

The helicopter turned ninety degrees to the left so that the AC could look back down the flight. Santini noticed that the last couple of choppers were still being loaded.

When all the men were aboard, the pilot faced north and began a slow takeoff run. He lifted gently, and they climbed into the brightening sky until they were wrapped in the dark grays of the clouds. Seconds later they burst through into the clear, bright morning sky.

MADDEN SAT IN THE COMMO BUNKER at Nha Trang, his head bowed, wishing he could get some sleep. He felt light-headed, and his eyes burned. The inside of his mouth tasted like a company had marched through it in muddy combat boots, taking time to wipe their feet. From a darkened corner came the snoring of one of the NCOs as he caught up on his sleep.

Slowly, stiffly, Madden got up and walked to the coffeepot. As it had been an hour earlier, it was still empty. No one had bothered to make coffee.

He stood there for a moment, holding the empty pot almost as if he believed his act would make coffee appear. Then he set it down and walked back to the counter. A sergeant sat in a pool of bright light reading a paperback novel.

Madden stared at him until he looked up. "Still nothing on the radios?"

"Sir, if we'd had any incoming traffic you'd have heard it."

Madden nodded, knowing it was true. There had been nothing from Plei Soi for hours, and the first relief column was out of touch as well. Madden had no idea what was happening, and no one would tell him. He rubbed his face, realizing how tired he was, but he knew he wouldn't be able to sleep.

He left the sergeant reading his paperback and walked to the other side of the bunker. The NCO who ran the switchboard wasn't sitting there. He waited impatiently for a moment and then shouted at the man with the novel, "Where the hell is the operator?"

"Had to go to the can, sir."

"Shit," said Madden. He paced until the man returned and said, "I want you to get on the lima lima to Moc Hoa and see if we can find out what's happening."

The sergeant sat down and looked at his switchboard. "I doubt they'll have anyone awake and on it, sir."

"I didn't ask for opinions. I told you to raise Moc Hoa," snapped Madden.

It took nearly five minutes, but the sergeant finally managed to raise someone at Moc Hoa. When the connection was made, Madden grabbed the headset and demanded, "Say status of relief column."

"Wait one."

Madden felt his head begin to throb. He knew that the man at the other end was checking with the officers to find out how much he should reveal over the land line. Everyone was so security conscious on some matters that it was impossible to get needed information, and yet, some of the time everyone was telling everyone everything he knew. His hand tightened on the phone until his knuckles were white and his fingers ached.

"Be advised," said the voice, "that the rescue column is en route with an ETA of ten to twenty minutes."

"Roger," said Madden. "Say status of Diablo."

"We have negative contact with Diablo."

That hadn't been unexpected given the situation. If the enemy hit the commo bunker with anything, or just managed to knock down the antennae, commo would cease. The land line was even more fragile than the radios.

"Roger," said Madden. "Please keep Werewolf advised of any change in status."

"Understood, Werewolf." The connection broke.

Madden handed the headset back to the sergeant. "Thanks for your help."

The NCO nodded and turned back to his equipment.

Madden returned to the radio counter but didn't say anything to the sergeant reading the book. He hoped Fulton and his team had managed to get out before the camp had fallen. He hoped Gerber and Fetterman had survived the assault. Rubbing his face again, trying to generate some feeling in it, he wished he knew what was happening in the field. That was the worst part of his job: knowing that someone was in trouble and that there wasn't a hell of a lot he could do about it.

GERBER LOOKED UP AGAIN. No longer was the inside of the redoubt a black mass. Now it was gray, dotted with dark shapes, the bodies of the men killed in the attack. The rubble that was strewn over the inside was taking on shape and form. The sun was coming up.

"We'd better make a break for it before it gets too light," said Fetterman.

Gerber didn't want to move. He wanted to find Fulton, sure that the Special Forces captain was still alive and trapped somewhere inside the redoubt, hiding from the enemy. But there was no way he could do that. The enemy was all around them now.

"Okay. Lead on. I'll bring up the rear."

Fetterman turned and disappeared into the darkness at the base of the wall. Gerber backed up slowly, watching the interior of the redoubt. He heard the sporadic firing of small arms, but it was nothing like the noise generated as the VC and NVA had attacked. There was an occasional explosion, most of them coming from outside the redoubt as the enemy slowly captured the last pockets of resistance.

Gerber reached the sandbagged wall and ducked. He slipped to one knee, facing into the redoubt, his weapon aimed into it. He listened to the scrambling sounds that were coming from inside the tunnel. There were grunts of effort and then a quiet voice said, "I think it's blocked."

Again Gerber glanced over his shoulder. "Can you dig your way through it?"

"Sure, Captain," said Fetterman. "But not before it's light out. We'd never reach the bunker line."

"Then we'll have to make a stand here." Gerber crawled into the open again. If they threw some sandbags up around them, they could create a bunker. It would provide some protection and would make it hard for the enemy to get at them. They could kill a number of the VC and NVA before they were killed themselves.

Fetterman stepped out and said, "We've a few grenades and a lot of ammo. If we can hold out until dark, then we might be able to slip away."

Gerber shook his head. "Don't think it's going to work, Tony. Unless they fuck around and don't make a good search of the camp, I'm afraid we've reached the end of the line here."

"So, what do you think?"

Gerber looked at the tired, dirty master sergeant and understood exactly what he meant. It came from working so closely with the man for so long. They could almost read each other's thoughts. It was a closeness many combat veterans refused to develop because they were afraid the other man would be killed, leaving the living soldier with a hole in his soul. Now it looked as if they both would die.

"I think," said Gerber, "I'll recommend they keep the camp open. Anything that Charlie wants this badly has to be kept open, if only to irritate him."

Before Fetterman could reply there was a cheer from outside the redoubt. A bugle blared and men shouted. It sounded as if the VC and NVA had started their victory celebration, although Gerber wasn't exactly sure what they would be celebrating. They had yet to secure the whole camp and they had failed to take any of the crew-served weapons or ammo points intact. Gerber had seen Fetterman blow up one weapon with a LAW and knew that Fulton had finally destroyed the ammo points with his command-detonated mines. And surveying the interior of the redoubt, he could see that the victory had been a costly one. There were a hundred or more dead VC and NVA soldiers lying around. No, it wasn't much of a victory.

But then, it wasn't much of a victory for the Americans, either. Sure, Gerber thought, they still held small portions of the camp, but that was only because the enemy hadn't gotten around to the mop-up. Right now it was almost a draw, with the VC and NVA ahead on points.

Gerber drove the thoughts from his mind. He wished it would rain again. The rain was now an ally, but the shower had ended as the sun appeared and was now little more than a fine mist. If they got a good, soaking thunderstorm with plenty of lightning, it might provide the cover they needed to break out of the camp.

"Tony, get someone working on clearing the tunnel, but don't break all the way through yet. We don't want to telegraph our moves to the enemy."

"Yes, sir."

"And when it's done, we'll lie low and see if we can't hide out until nightfall. Then we'll have the chance to get out of here."

Fetterman nodded and leaned his weapon against the wall of the tunnel. Gerber noticed that he had lost the grease gun sometime during the night and had replaced it with an M-16. Not a good weapon for hand-to-hand fighting, but not a bad one when the enemy stormed the walls.

No, Gerber didn't think they'd be able to avoid the enemy until nightfall and he didn't think there would be a rescue attempt, not without radio contact. And Gerber had no idea where the radios were.

12

ORBITING NORTH OF
TAY NINH

All Santini could see below him was a sea of gray-black clouds. Above him, the sky was a deep dark blue, but below, a boiling mass of energy. He kept watch, but the helicopters never came close to it. They orbited as the sun climbed higher and higher, and Santini became convinced they couldn't get to Camp A-337 before it was overrun.

The crew chief leaned around the transmission wall and tapped Santini on the shoulder. When he had Santini's attention, he stripped his flight helmet and yelled for Santini to put it on.

Over the intercom the AC said, "I've got your Major Winger on the radio here, and he wants to talk to you. Be advised we have negative radio connect with the camp and apparently haven't had any messages from it in two or three hours."

Santini nodded and then reached up to flip the switch on the radio control head. "Go."

"Roger. We have negative contact with Diablo Six."

"Roger that."

"Mission should be aborted until contact is established."

Santini knew Winger wasn't ordering the abort, but was asking for assistance. Winger was unfamiliar with the camp and was asking for advice. Santini wasn't that familiar with it, either. All he knew was that an A-Detachment was on the ground, augmented by two additional Special Forces soldiers. In each instance where a camp had been overrun, the majority of Americans had managed to get themselves out. Maybe some of them died in the defense, or in the escape, but no whole detachments had been killed. It was important that they get to the camp because there would be men on the ground who needed their help.

"Can we recon?" asked Santini.

There was a momentary hesitation and then, "Roger. We'll recon."

Santini leaned back against the ragged, gray sound-proofing and waited. Every second was important, but they couldn't land if the enemy held the whole camp, not without a much larger force. Then, off to the west, he saw another helicopter company, not a small unit like the one he was in, but a larger one with fifteen or twenty ships. That meant an additional hundred and fifty or two hundred men. And to the east was a third company. Another hundred and fifty men. Now the landing force was big enough for anything.

Over the radio he heard, "Bravo Three, this is Six. Recon shows enemy forces are inside wire, but there still seems to be resistance. We're going in."

Santini wanted to cheer. He sat up straighter and took off the helmet, handed it to the crew chief. He checked his weapon, chambered a round and then made sure the safety was on. There was a change in the noise of the engine, and they rolled out. They flew straight and level for several minutes and then a gunship appeared in front of them, punching up through the clouds and then spinning around. That ship disappeared into the cloud cover again.

Now they all slipped into the clouds and the wall of gray. Santini strained to hear something, anything, but the sound of the helicopters and the popping of the rotor blades drowned everything out. He flinched once and felt his muscles tighten. Consciously he relaxed and then tensed again. His knuckles turned white where he gripped the weapon, and he feared the helicopters would fly into one another.

But they broke through the clouds about a thousand feet above the ground. Santini sat up and stared out the front of the chopper. In the distance, through a haze of mist, he could see the outline of the camp. Smoke filled the air above it.

Suddenly they plunged to the ground so that they were only a few feet above it. As they raced over the rice paddies, the rotor wash created changing patterns on the surface of the water. When they neared the camp, it began to sparkle and shimmer as the enemy opened fire. Tracers flashed by, but everyone seemed to ignore them. Santini tore his eyes away, convinced he would die if he watched the tracers. He turned his head and looked at the men in the chopper with him.

He couldn't read much from them. They were grim-faced and quiet, but that meant nothing. He stared into the eyes of a Vietnamese sergeant. The man grinned, showing pointed, yellowed teeth. Then he turned to look out the cargo compartment door as if anticipating the coming fight.

Suddenly the door guns opened fire. The ruby tracers walked into the camp and began ripping into the bunker line. Heavy enemy fire was directed at them, but the rounds missed the choppers.

Then, as they raced past the east side of the camp, the helicopter flared and the door guns fell silent. Santini lost sight of everything except the clouds overhead, now visible through the windshield. The pilot leveled the skids and the aircraft dropped to the ground. As it touched down, the Vietnamese strikers leaped into the grass and rice paddies. Bullets began to kick up the dirt around them and splash into the water.

Santini leaped out of the cargo compartment, stumbled in the water and fell to his knees. As he got up, the helicopters lifted off and the door guns began to fire again, trying to suppress the enemy in the camp.

Winger ran toward the road that led into the camp, shouting, "Follow me. Let's go. Let's go!" He fired from his hip and ran.

Santini sprinted after him with the Vietnamese stringing out behind them. He felt a roar bubbling in his throat as he leaped over the bodies of the dead VC and NVA, which littered the ground outside the camp.

At the bunker line, they spread out as firing erupted along the enemy-held line. M-16s taken off the dead strikers, M-60s captured when the line had collapsed, were turned against the Americans. There were pops and then explosions as grenades were launched from captured M-79s. Soviet-made RPDs and AKs joined in.

But neither Winger nor Santini slowed. They ran along the road through the gaps in the wire blown by the VC, then leaped to the gate. Santini dropped to the ground there and began firing at the enemy. He saw VC and NVA running inside the camp and shot at them.

Grenades began to explode on the bunker line as the Vietnamese attacked.

Then more firing broke out from the other side of the camp as the assault force there hit the ground. The noise crescendoed to a roar like that of surf on the beach, and Santini knew the enemy wouldn't be able to withstand the American onslaught.

GERBER KEPT WATCH inside the redoubt as Fetterman scrambled to build them a bunker. The higher the sun rose, the more the firing around them continued to drop off. Now it sounded as if snipers were trying to pick off a few troops, or as if the VC were trying to kill the last of the survivors. Then, in the distance, Gerber thought he heard the sound of helicopters. One had flown over earlier, but it had been too dark to see much, and Gerber hadn't held much hope that it would bring help. The VC and NVA hadn't shot at it, and if Gerber had been thinking faster, he would have.

But that all seemed to be in the past now. The noise of the choppers grew, and he knew that an assault force was inbound. They would be ready, he was sure, because they would try to raise Diablo Six on the radio. When that failed, they would expect the worst.

Over his shoulder he said, "Tony. I think help's on the way."

Fetterman came out of the darkness of the tunnel, stopped and listened. "Yeah!" He leaned back and grabbed his weapon.

Firing broke out to the south. At first it was sporadic, but then everyone got into it. Gerber kept his eyes on the sky and finally spotted the helicopters. The closer they got to the camp, the more the shooting intensified. VC and NVA inside the redoubt crowded to the east side.

They aimed their weapons into the gray morning sky and began to shoot.

Gerber didn't wait. He threw his weapon to his shoulder and aimed at the backs of the enemy soldiers. He pulled the trigger rapidly and watched the VC begin to collapse. Two of them rolled down the slope of the embankment, but the rest of the soldiers didn't seem to notice.

To his left, Fetterman joined him, as did Timmons. More of the enemy died. Finally one of the Vietcong turned and saw that they were being attacked from the rear. He opened fire, his rounds striking the sandbags between Gerber and Fetterman.

Gerber shifted position and continued to fire. His first round struck the man high. He threw his AK into the air and screamed, clutching his chest. As he fell, several of his friends turned toward him.

Fetterman dropped two of them, but then they spotted the tiny band of Americans. One of them yelled and more of the VC spun around. When they did, the top of the redoubt was raked with machine gun fire that could have come from the choppers, or from the attackers leaping out of them. Now the NVA found themselves caught in a cross fire.

Some of them dived for cover near the ruins of the dispensary. One of them stood to throw a grenade, but Gerber shot him. He lobbed the grenade as he died, but it exploded harmlessly.

The firefight increased. Gerber kept shooting on semi-auto, aiming at the men hidden by the dispensary, pulling the trigger rapidly. His bullets struck the rubble, kicking it up. He saw another man fall. Two tried to run toward the gate of the redoubt where the jeep and the barrels and sandbags blocked it. One of them jumped up, was hit and fell into the redoubt. The other was confused. He threw his weapon on the ground and lifted his hands to surrender. He looked around wildly, but couldn't find anyone to accept the surrender. Finally he dived to the ground and tried to roll under the jeep, attempting to hide there.

Outside, the firing continued to increase, first to the east, and then to the west—short, quiet bursts of firing initially and then sustained firing from M-16s that quickly became a roar.

Suddenly the air above them was filled with American and Vietnamese bullets directed at the NVA and VC soldiers who were inside the camp. The enemy in the redoubt were no longer worried about the three men in the tiny bunker. They were looking to escape from the camp. They were running around, looking for hiding places or for ways to get out. Several of them tried to climb over the jeep and were killed immediately. Another dropped his weapon and threw up his hands, yelling *"Chieu Hoi,"* but was shot and killed.

Gerber watched the destruction of the NVA. The coordinated defense fell apart as the enemy tried to get out alive. They were throwing down their weapons to surrender now that they were caught without hope of escape. They clustered in the center of the redoubt, away from the walls and waited for someone to take charge.

Gerber was tempted to crawl from his cover and do just that, but he didn't want to take the chance. If some of the NVA decided to make a last stand, Gerber didn't want to get killed in it. Instead, he yelled at the men in Vietnamese, "Keep your hands up and get to your knees."

SANTINI GOT TO HIS FEET and ran forward through the broken main gate. He turned right and dived for cover at the edge of one of the ruined bunkers there. Forcing himself closer to the sandbag walls, he searched for the enemy. For a moment no one was visible. He could hear the sounds of AKs and RPDs. Chicom grenades were detonating all around. He thought he saw a muzzle-flash and fired at it.

The response was immediate. Slugs stitched a line near him. A sandbag exploded, raining dirt on him, choking him. Santini threw a hand over the receiver group of his weapon as he coughed and spit, trying to get the dirt out of his mouth. He rubbed his eyes and felt a burning sensation as the grit scratched him.

Santini lowered his head and sucked at the air. It smelled of mud and tasted of grit. More bullets struck the side of the bunker. Santini felt the impact.

Finally, through the tears caused by the dirt, he could see again. A blurred image of men moving, running, falling. He rubbed at his eyes and stared. There was a man in black pajamas sprinting to the north, and Santini fired at him. The man was lifted off his feet and tossed into the mud.

Then Santini was on his feet, running, dodging a pile of equipment dropped by the fleeing NVA. Skidding to a halt, he fell to one knee and fired at the enemy on the north, then rolled to the right through the mud and fired again.

From the northeastern corner of the bunker line a machine gun opened up. Bullets buried themselves in the mud near him. Santini aimed and returned fire, but the machine gun continued to hammer away.

Several of the strikers turned to shoot at the enemy position. One threw grenades that landed short, tossing

mud and water into the air and hiding the bunker behind clouds of dark smoke. Through it all the machine
gun continued to fire, its tracers dancing in the gray mist.

Then one man, holding a LAW, ran by him. The man
leaped over a barrel and slid to a stop with a splash of
water and a spray of mud. He pulled the cotter pins,
opened the weapon and then aimed. Before he fired, he
glanced to the rear to make sure no one would be in-
jured by the backblast. When he saw that no one was
behind him, he scrambled to his knees and aimed. As
he fired, the machine gun nailed him, killing him.

But the missile was true. It buried itself in the sandbags of the bunker and exploded. At first the bunker
seemed to tremble and the machine gun continued to
chug, but then it shrank and blew up with a rumbling
bang and a flash of bright orange fire.

As the debris began to rain on the ground, two men
were up and running toward the bunker, firing from the
hip. Another sprinted to the man who had fired the LAW
and turned him over. Blood covered his chest, staining
his OD fatigues crimson. He was obviously dead.

Santini watched as the medic dropped the man into the
mud. Not much respect for a soldier who had given his
life to save others, he thought. After the camp was secured, Santini vowed he would return and try to find out
the man's name. Then he was up again, moving toward
the redoubt.

As he hurdled one of the fifty-five-gallon drums, he
heard firing to the right. He felt a white-hot burning in
his chest, and a black curtain began to descend over his
eyes. Momentarily confused, Santini knew he was falling. He didn't know that he'd hit the ground, and his last
conscious thought was that you weren't supposed to hear
the one that got you.

"IT SOUNDS LIKE THE RELIEF COLUMN is in the camp," said Timmons.

"Right," agreed Gerber, "but we'll stay right here until we see some of our people."

Fetterman added, "We're safe here. Until we get some indication of how things are going, it would be stupid to risk our necks. We might run into something that we know nothing about, but that the relief force does."

"I wasn't suggesting—"

"There," said Gerber, pointing. "That's someone from the Mike Force."

And then more men came boiling over the top of the jeep and rubble that had been thrown into the gateway. Gerber scrambled from his cover, waving his hands to attract their attention. "Don't shoot. Don't shoot."

The prisoners all fell to their stomachs, almost as if they had been ordered to, their hands on their heads. A couple of the strikers, rushing into the redoubt, fired wild shots, but then dropped to the ground, their weapons at the ready.

Gerber shouted, "Take charge of the prisoners. Let's go." He turned and grabbed Fetterman's hand, helping the master sergeant from their cover.

Timmons stayed crouching in the trench, his back braced against the wet dirt of the sides, saying over and over, "All right. All right." He pounded his fist into his thigh sharply as he spoke.

A moment later an American officer wearing a green beret leaped to the hood of the jeep and dropped to the ground. He stood quietly for a moment, taking in the scene, and then started across the compound. When he was close, he asked, "Are you Fulton?"

Gerber held out a hand. "Gerber. Lost track of Fulton."

There was a single shot, and both men dived to the ground. Fetterman returned the fire quickly and then grinned at the two officers. "If you gentlemen are through playing Stanley and Livingstone..."

Gerber saw the point. He dropped back into the trench and then moved along it. He rested his arms on the sandbags that formed the top of the trench and stood studying the strikers. They were moving among the prisoners, taking everything they could, ignoring the shooting that was going on outside the redoubt.

"Major," said Gerber, "how bad is it out there?"

Winger rubbed his face and then wiped his hand on the front of his fatigues. "I think most of the enemy fled before we were on short final. Some mopping up to do, but I think Charlie got out when the sun came up. Or maybe he got out when he heard the helicopters. We ran into the rear guard."

"Okay," said Gerber. "There are things that need to be done. Tony, I want you to find out who's still alive. We'll need a roster of the men who've been killed or are missing to report to Saigon."

"Vietnamese and American?"

"No," said Gerber. "You worry about the Americans. Sergeant Timmons, you get with the Vietnamese and find the highest-ranking man left alive. You'll need to find out who's been killed and who's been wounded."

"Yes, sir."

"I've got to coordinate the mop-up," Winger said, interrupting. "It shouldn't take long."

Gerber nodded and then listened. The firing that had been heavy was now little more than occasional shots. The sound that had filled the air was now gone. Gerber looked at the sky, a roiling mass of clouds that threatened more rain. There was a light breeze that smelled of rain and dampness and maybe of death. There was a chill in the air, unusual for this part of the tropics.

"Christ!" said Gerber. He realized that he had managed to survive against the odds and that by noon he would be in Saigon. He could take a hot shower, either alone or with company, depending on how he felt, eat a good solid meal and be as safe as if he were in the World. He could sit in a hotel room, his feet up, and watch television if he felt like it.

"Christ," he repeated. "What a night."

Fetterman appeared beside him. "You going to recommend they close the camp now?"

Gerber studied the master sergeant—a muddy, dirty man with a heavy stubble on his face. There were dark circles under his eyes, giving his face an almost skull-like appearance. He grinned at Fetterman almost cheerfully. "What do you think?"

"I think we should keep it open."

"I do, too. Now."

13

Gerber sat at one end of the conference table, looking at the pitcher surrounded by water glasses. He had been in Saigon only long enough for a quick shower and a change of clothes. Almost as soon as Winger had thought the camp had been retaken, he had ordered Gerber and Fetterman to a chopper. They were ferried to Tay Ninh, put on another helicopter and flown to Tan Son Nhut. At Hotel Three they were met by Major O'Herlihy and taken to their hotel.

But Gerber didn't feel refreshed by the shower, nor did he feel clean. While Fetterman had been using the shower, Gerber had tried to find Morrow, but she hadn't been in her room and the other press people at her bureau didn't know where she was. She was out on assignment was the only thing they would tell him.

For some reason Gerber felt very disappointed. He wanted a chance to talk to her and let her know he was all right. Given the situation, he doubted she knew what had happened, and he wanted to tell her about it before someone else did. He was positive the press would be waiting to pounce on the story, and if he could talk to her first, it might save her some unnecessary worrying.

Although there were several men already in the conference room, they were all quiet, waiting for the arrival of the general. Gerber glanced at Fetterman who sat to the side, his head against the wall, his eyes closed and his hands folded in his lap. Gerber was amazed at Fetterman's ability to relax anywhere at anytime, taking every opportunity to rest because he never knew when he would have to stay awake for two or three days.

The door opened and a staff officer entered. "Gentlemen, General Davidson."

Each man got to his feet and waited as the general entered and sat down. Once he was comfortable, he surveyed the room and then said, "Please be seated."

He waited for the staff to settle down and then looked at Gerber. "Got yourself in the middle of a mess, didn't you, Captain?"

Gerber couldn't help grinning. "Seemed to have stepped into it, General. But then I was ordered into the field to survey the situation."

"You have a written report on the attack?"

"No, sir. I can put together a report later, but we didn't get back to Saigon until an hour ago."

O'Herlihy spoke up. "What were casualties like?"

"Three Americans killed, three missing and four wounded. The Vietnamese camp commander, Captain Minh, is missing, too."

"Captain Fulton?"

"He's one of the missing. When we left the camp, no one had found him or his body. It's the same with Sergeant Miller and Sergeant Clements."

"You say this Minh is missing?" asked one of the officers. "Maybe he went over during the attack."

"No," snapped Gerber. "I know Captain Minh. He's as trustworthy as anyone at the camp. Like Captain Fulton and the others, he's missing in action."

"Shit," said a colonel. "Three more missing in action."

"Not to mention the killed and wounded," said Gerber, staring at the man.

"Okay," interrupted Davidson. "The main question is whether or not we should close that base."

Gerber glanced at Fetterman and then said, "When I was on my first tour in Vietnam, we had a similar situation. My camp was built right in the middle of a supply line for the enemy. Here in Saigon some of the generals wanted to close the base, claiming it was too expensive to keep it open. We weathered a full-scale NVA attack and the brass in Saigon—"

"The point, Captain."

"The point is that if the VC and NVA want us out of there that badly, then we should stay. Anytime we create a camp that they hit with that kind of force means that we've done something to really piss them off."

"But this camp no longer actually exists, does it?" asked O'Herlihy.

Gerber turned and faced the officer. "There'd have to be some rebuilding, yes, but that's not the point. The point is that the NVA attacked with an eye to push us out of that camp. To my way of thinking, that means we have to rebuild. We have to put a large force in there because it's going to fuck up the enemy and that's the point of everything we do."

Davidson looked at his staff but didn't speak.

"General," said Gerber. "It takes a day to put a fire support base in. One day. And that's from bare ground. If you don't want a Special Forces camp, then put in a fire support base and dare the VC to take it."

"There is another consideration," said Davidson. "With this latest assault I think we can assume that the intel reports we've received about a Communist buildup are accurate. Charlie is moving larger numbers of people into South Vietnam. He's getting good support from the North Vietnamese."

"General," said Fetterman, "if I may interrupt."

"Go ahead, Sergeant."

"Thank you, General." He faced the assembled staff officers and said, "There's something that I've observed over the past several weeks. We have large numbers of NVA working with the VC. They've infiltrated the VC ranks. No, that's not quite right. Infiltrated isn't the right word."

He stopped and thought about it and then continued. "The NVA are putting men into squad-sized VC units. They give up their NVA uniforms and dress in the black pajamas of the VC."

"What's the point here?" asked O'Herlihy.

"The point, Major, is that something big is coming. We have increased traffic, but we don't have increased contact. The enemy's lying low with a few notable exceptions. The Hobo Woods was a mistake, but this attack wasn't."

"Sergeant, you're taking a long time to get to the point of all this."

"Sorry, General. This attack was designed to reduce the camp by storm. It wasn't designed to take the camp because once they did that, they made no real effort to hold it. Some of them got caught by the rapid response of the Mike Force, but the majority of the enemy got away. The counterattack didn't matter to them. They had gained their objective."

Gerber turned and looked at Fetterman, and suddenly he understood exactly what the master sergeant was saying. He took over. "You see, General, they didn't plan to hold it. They wanted to destroy it so that it wouldn't be there for a couple of weeks. They know how we operate."

"And, General," said Fetterman, "they apparently wiped out a hamlet because it happened to be in the wrong place. Sergeant Timmons of the A-Detachment in Plei Soi noted that the destruction of the hamlet wasn't done by American or Vietnamese forces. The NVA and VC did it, and I think they did it because they didn't want anyone living on an important route for them."

"Important in what way?" asked O'Herlihy.

Fetterman shrugged. "Who knows? I just know the enemy is making moves that aren't random. There's a pattern to this. They refrain from engaging in their normal harassment activities, but they make a major push to remove a specific Special Forces camp. It's no accident."

"Which means," said Gerber, "that we have to get that camp rebuilt and functioning in a matter of hours if we can. Hell, General, the basic groundwork is done. The structures on the camp have been burned and many of the bunkers were blown up, but that could be repaired quickly. I think Sergeant Fetterman is right. We need to get someone in there quickly because the enemy is planning something big in the very near future."

"Gentlemen?" said the General, inviting debate. And debate they did. They argued about the logistics for a base that close to Cambodia. They argued about the need for the men to be closer to Saigon because that would be where an enemy thrust, if it came, would be directed. Even if Fetterman was right, the enemy would still move on Saigon, so maybe it made sense to abandon the site. They argued for nearly an hour, most of the time about things that had no relevance to the base. Davidson finally ended it by asking, "What do you think, Master Sergeant?"

Fetterman got to his feet and stared the general in the eye. "I still have to say that if Charlie wanted us out of there so badly, then we should stay put."

Davidson nodded and said, "Thank you. Captain Gerber, you and Sergeant Fetterman are dismissed."

Gerber stood up and moved to the door. He stopped, looked back as if he wanted to say something and then decided against it. He moved into the hallway.

When Fetterman joined him, he asked, "What do you think they'll do, Captain?"

"I think they'll argue about it the rest of the afternoon and then Davidson will decide to leave some kind of force there for the reasons that we gave him. They'll do it to fuck up the enemy and for no other reason. And the staff will go along with it because Davidson wants it that way."

"Good."

SANTINI WAS AWARE OF A PAIN in his shoulder, a dull ache that seemed to radiate outward from a single, white-hot point, an ache that infected his chest as he breathed and blossomed in his stomach. He thought he might throw up, then figured he wouldn't and finally decided he would. Instead, he lay on his back and opened his eyes.

Above him was the white of corrugated tin. Cool air blew at him from somewhere, and he slowly became aware that he wasn't alone. There were men in other beds around him, wounded men with bandages around arms or legs or their heads. Most of them were awake, reading magazines as nurses moved among them. When he saw all that, he breathed a sigh of relief. If he was in any danger, he would be in a room by himself, or on a Medevac plane heading for Japan.

He turned his head and saw a pretty dark-haired nurse staring at him. She grinned and said, "You lied to me. You didn't write."

Santini looked at the massive bandage on his shoulder and said weakly, "I can't write real well."

"This is a hell of a way to get a date. You could have asked for one on the chopper, but no, you have to find a fancy way to get my attention."

"Worked, didn't it?"

She took his hand and squeezed it. "Worked real good. Now you've got to get some rest, but I want you to buy me a dinner just as soon as you can."

"On the weekend," said Santini, rising to the occasion. "If we don't have to dance."

"You got it. Now I've got to get back to work. I'll stop by later to see how you are."

"Thanks." He watched her as she left the ward and wondered where she got fatigues that were that tight. Not that he was complaining.

MINH SAT QUIETLY in the midafternoon heat, watching the enemy pass by him. He was hidden deep in a clump of bamboo and leafy ferns, afraid to move and almost afraid to breathe. After he had escaped from the camp, he had made his way north, away from the camp where he could still hear shooting. He had been forced to the north by the enemy as they had returned to their rally points and staging areas.

In the dark and rain he was able to avoid them easily, with one minor exception. Working his way through a thick clump of trees, he fell over a man who was sitting, playing with his weapon. The surprised Vietcong said something in Vietnamese. Minh responded and then drove his knife into the man, forcing it up under his breastbone to destroy the heart. The enemy died without knowing why.

Minh scrambled away then, forgetting for a moment about noise discipline. He just wanted to put distance between himself and the dead man. If his friends found the body, they would be hard-pressed to figure out what had happened. All they would know was that their comrade was dead by violence.

Near dawn Minh slowed down and then stopped to rest. When the rain let up, he could no longer hear firing at the camp, but that didn't mean much. He could be so far away that the sound didn't make it to him. The wind, coming from the west, would blow the noise to the east, making it hard for him to hear.

Behind him, he still heard the noise of the enemy force. They were beginning to scatter into smaller units so that the Americans, if they pursued, wouldn't luck into a regiment. They might find a platoon, if they were fortunate. That meant Minh had to keep moving; he didn't want to be found.

By midmorning he was worn out. Sweat was pouring off him and he was beginning to dehydrate badly. Since he had found it necessary to escape from the camp in a hurry, he had taken almost no equipment or supplies. He did carry an empty canteen stolen from the body of a dead NVA, but he had finished the water the moment he had found the canteen.

Now, sitting in the bush, he slowly and carefully reached out to roll leaves into tubes. By tilting them upward, he was able to catch a few drops of water in his mouth, but there just wasn't enough to quench his thirst. The process, which had to be slow so that he didn't alert any enemy soldiers who might be near, kept his mind off the disaster of the night before, kept him from thinking about the destruction of his camp and the deaths of his fellow soldiers.

Finally he realized there was nothing he could do until nightfall. He would have to stay hidden until dark. Then, believing that the VC and NVA would continue traveling north, deeper into the jungle, or west, heading for the sanctuaries of Cambodia, he would turn back south. He would have to be careful because there would probably be patrols of strikers and American Special Forces men out, but he should be able to make contact with them.

He slipped deeper into the bush, huddling closer to its base. With the sweat dripping from him, and the sound of flying insects in his ears, he closed his eyes. If he could sleep, the night would come much faster. If he could sleep, he wouldn't be conscious of the horror that had overrun his camp the night before. If only he could sleep.

GERBER SAT in the air-conditioned luxury of one of the many bars in the Oriental Hotel, sipping a beer and waiting for Robin to meet him. Fetterman had positioned himself with his back to the door, a half-finished beer in front of him.

"You know, Captain, that was a little closer than I care to get."

"Yes," said Gerber. "I think, though, that we should go back out there as soon as we can. I'd like to look over the camp and see if we can find Fulton and Minh and the others. Get a better reading on what happened to our people."

"I understand, sir, but this happens whenever the VC make a concentrated push against one of our camps."

"That doesn't mean I have to let it go until we've exhausted every opportunity to find our men," said Gerber. He picked up his beer and took a deep pull.

Fetterman nodded. "Well, as soon as you get the transport arranged, let me know. I'll go out with you. There are a number of things I want to explore, anyway."

"Funny about Minh," said Gerber. "I thought he was indestructible."

"Just remember, sir, that Captain Minh can take care of himself, and no one's identified his body. I wouldn't be surprised to hear he's still alive."

"Yeah. That's why I haven't proposed a toast to him. I don't want to drink to a dead man and find out he's still alive."

"Then to his health," said Fetterman.

Gerber lifted his glass. "To his health." As he drained the last of his beer, he saw Robin approaching. He stood and waved at her.

When she was near, Fetterman said, "Afternoon, Robin. Nice to see you again. If you'll excuse me, I've a couple of errands to run."

She smiled at the master sergeant. "Don't be ridiculous. Stay and have another beer with us. I'm sure Mack won't mind."

"I don't know," said Gerber in mock seriousness. "I have to hang around with him all the time. Well, I guess it's all right. But just one beer."

Morrow sat down, and no one spoke for a moment. A waitress appeared, took the order and retreated. As she left, Morrow turned toward Gerber, leaned her elbows on the table and rested her chin on her hands. "So, what have you two been up to in the past few hours?"

Gerber glanced at Fetterman. "Nothing important. Just out on a survey of a camp that MACV has been thinking of closing."

"Sounds like there's a real story there," she said sarcastically.

"Oh, yes," added Fetterman. "But then, everyone seemed to think we should leave it right where it is."

The waitress returned and put a beer in front of each of them.

Morrow tasted the brew and made a face at it. "I don't know why I ordered this. I don't like beer."

"It's an acquired taste." Fetterman drank deeply and set his glass down. He looked from Morrow to Gerber and then at his glass. "I feel like a fifth wheel here. If you'll excuse me."

"Tony, finish your beer first," Gerber told him.

"Sure, Captain." Fetterman picked up his glass, raised it to his lips and chugged it. Then he set the empty glass on the table. "Finished. Now if you'll excuse me, I've things to do. Good to see you again, Miss Morrow."

"Good to see you, Tony."

"I'll see you tomorrow, sir." Fetterman turned, waved at the waitress and headed toward the door.

"He didn't have to run off," said Morrow.

"No, he didn't," responded Gerber, "but then, the master sergeant is a class individual. He knows we'll want to be alone."

"And do we?" asked Morrow.

Gerber leaned forward and took her hand. "Of course we do. First, we'll finish our beers and then we'll find something else to do."

"You take a lot for granted, sir."

"Then we'll finish our beers and I'll run over to MACV to see what's happening and you can return to work."

Now she squeezed his hand. "I didn't mean that you weren't right, just that you took a lot for granted." She rocked back in her chair and studied Gerber for a moment. She cocked her head to one side and asked, "Did I miss something?"

"What do you mean?"

"I mean, are you okay? You look a little . . . I don't know. Tired? Sick?"

For an instant he was tempted to tell her all about the night before, about the VC and NVA overrunning the camp, but he didn't. She was a journalist, and although he knew he could trust her, the prevailing attitude at MACV was that nothing was to be shared with the press. They wanted everyone to believe that the war was winding down, and the story of a nearly successful, hell, a successful assault on a Special Forces camp would make the press ask too many questions.

So he just said, "I've been up all night, then was recalled and only had time to take a shower and change my clothes. I haven't had a chance to go to bed yet."

Morrow stood, ignoring the half-finished beer in front of her. She tugged at Gerber's hand. "Then, by all means, let's go to bed."

"I thought you'd never ask." He stood, dropped a small bundle of bills on the table, then repeated, "I thought you'd never ask."

GLOSSARY

AC—Aircraft commander. The pilot in charge of the aircraft.

AFVN—Armed Forces radio and television network in Vietnam. Army PFC Pat Sajak was probably the most memorable of AFVN's DJs with his loud and long, "GOOOOOOOOOOOOD MORNing, Vietnam!" The spinning Wheel of Fortune gives no clues about his whereabouts today.

AK-47—Soviet-made assault rifle normally used by the North Vietnamese and the Vietcong.

AO—Area of Operations.

AO DAI—Long dresslike garment, split up the sides and worn over pants.

AP ROUNDS—Armor-piercing ammunition.

APU—Auxiliary Power Unit. An outside source of power used to start aircraft engines.

ARVN—Army of the Republic of Vietnam. A South Vietnamese soldier. Also known as Marvin Arvin.

BISCUIT—C-rations.

BODY COUNT—Number of enemy killed, wounded or captured during an operation. Used by Saigon and Washington as a means of measuring progress of the war.

BOOM BOOM—Term used by Vietnamese prostitutes in selling their product.

BOONDOGGLE—Any military operation that hasn't been completely thought out. An operation that is ridiculous.

BOONIE HATS—Soft cap worn by grunts in the field when they were not wearing their steel pot.

BUSHMASTER—Jungle warfare expert or soldier skilled in jungle navigation. Also a large deadly snake not common to Vietnam but mighty tasty.

C AND C—Command and Control aircraft that circled overhead to direct the combined air and ground operations.

CARIBOU—Cargo transport plane.

CHINOOK—Army Aviation twin-engine helicopter. A CH-47. Also known as a shit hook.

CHOCK—Refers to the number of the aircraft in the flight. Chock Three is the third. Chock Six is the sixth.

CLAYMORE—Antipersonnel mine that fires seven hundred and fifty steel balls with a lethal range of fifty meters.

CLOSE AIR SUPPORT—Use of airplanes and helicopters to fire on enemy units near friendlies.

CO CONG—Female Vietcong.

DAI UY—Vietnamese army rank equivalent to captain.

DEROS—Date Estimated Return from Overseas Services.

E AND E—Escape and Evasion.

FEET WET—Term used by pilots to describe flight over water.

FIVE—Radio call sign for the executive officer of a unit.

FOX MIKE—FM radio.

FNG—Fucking New Guy.

FREEDOM BIRD—Name given to any aircraft that took troops out of Vietnam. Usually referred to the commercial jet flights that took men back to the World.

GARAND—M-1 rifle that was replaced by the M-14. Issued to the Vietnamese early in the war.

GO-TO-HELL-RAG—Towel or any large cloth worn around the neck by grunts.

GRAIL—NATO name for the shoulder-fired SA-7 surface-to-air missile.

GUARD THE RADIO—A term that means standing by in the commo bunker and listening for messages.

GUIDELINE—NATO name for the SA-2 surface-to-air missiles.

GUNSHIP—Armed helicopter or cargo plane that carries weapons instead of cargo.

HE—High-explosive ammunition.

HOOTCH—Almost any shelter, from temporary to long-term.

HORN—Term that referred to a specific kind of radio operations that used satellites to rebroadcast messages.

HORSE—See *Biscuit*.

HOTEL THREE—Helicopter landing area at Saigon's Tan Son Nhut Airport.

HUEY—UH-1 helicopter.

IN-COUNTRY—Term used to refer to American troops operating in South Vietnam. They were all in-country.

INTELLIGENCE—Any information about enemy operations. It can include troop movements, weapons capabilities, biographies of enemy commanders and general information about terrain features. It is any information that would be useful in planning a mission.

KA-BAR—Type of military combat knife.

KIA—Killed In Action. (Since the U.S. was not engaged in a declared war, the use of the term KIA was not authorized. KIA came to mean enemy dead. Americans were KHA, or Killed In Hostile Action.)

KLICK—A thousand meters. A kilometer.

LIMA LIMA—Land Line. Refers to telephone communications between two points on the ground.

LLDB—Luc Luong Dac Biet. The South Vietnamese Special Forces. Sometimes referred to as the Look Long, Duck Back.

LP—Listening Post. A position outside the perimeter manned by a couple of people to give advance warning of enemy activity.

LZ—Landing Zone.

M-3—Also known as a Grease Gun. A .45-caliber submachine gun that was favored in World War II by

GIs. Its slow rate of fire meant the barrel didn't rise. As well, the user didn't burn through his ammo as fast as he did with some of his other weapons.

M-14—Standard rifle of the U.S., eventually replaced by the M-16. It fired the standard NATO round— 7.62 mm.

M-16—Became the standard infantry weapon of the Vietnam War. It fired 5.56 mm ammunition.

M-79—Short-barreled, shoulder-fired weapon that fires a 40 mm grenade. These can be high explosives, white phosphorus or canister.

MACV—Military Assistance Command, Vietnam, replaced MAAG in 1964.

MEDEVAC—Also called Dust-Off. A helicopter used to take the wounded to medical facilities.

MIA—Missing In Action.

NCO—A noncommissioned officer. A noncom. A sergeant.

NCOIC—NCO In Charge. The senior NCO in a unit, detachment or patrol.

NEXT—The man who said it was his turn next to be rotated home. See *Short*.

NINETEEN—Average age of combat soldier in Vietnam, as opposed to twenty-six in World War II.

NOUC MAM—Foul-smelling sauce used by Vietnamese.

NVA—North Vietnamese Army. Also used to designate a soldier from North Vietnam.

P (PIASTER)—Basic monetary unit in South Vietnam worth slightly less than a penny.

PETA-PRIME—Tarlike substance that melted in the heat of the day to become a sticky black nightmare that clung to boots, clothes and equipment. It was used to hold down the dust during the dry season.

PETER PILOT—Copilot in a helicopter.

PLF—Parachute Landing Fall. The roll used by parachutists on landing.

POW—Prisoner Of War.

PRC-10—Portable radio.

PRC-25—Lighter portable radio that replaced the PRC-10.

PULL PITCH—Term used by helicopter pilots that means they are going to take off.

PUNJI STAKE—Sharpened bamboo hidden to penetrate the foot. Sometimes dipped in feces.

RINGKNOCKER—Graduate of a military academy. The term refers to the ring worn by all graduates.

RON—Remain Overnight. Term used by flight crews to indicate a flight that would last longer than a day.

RPD—Soviet 7.62 mm light machine gun.

RTO—Radio Telephone Operator. The radio man of a unit.

SA-2—Surface-to-air missile fired from a fixed site. It is a radar-guided missile that is nearly thirty-five feet long.

SA-7—Surface-to-air missile that is shoulder-fired and has infrared homing.

SAFE AREA—Selected Area For Evasion. It doesn't mean that the area is safe from the enemy, only that the terrain, location, or local population make the area a good place for escape and evasion.

SAM TWO—Refers to the SA-2 Guideline.

SAR—Search And Rescue. SAR forces would be the people involved in search-and-rescue missions.

SHIT HOOK—Name applied by troops to the Chinook helicopter because of all the ''shit'' stirred up by the massive rotors.

SHORT—Term used by everyone in Vietnam to tell all who would listen that his tour was almost over.

SHORT FINAL—The moment just before a helicopter touched down.

SHORT-TIMER—Person who had been in Vietnam for nearly a year and who would be rotated back to the World soon. When the DEROS (Date of Estimated Return from Overseas) was the shortest in the unit, the person was said to be next.

SIX—Radio call sign for the unit commander.

SKS—Soviet-made carbine.

SMG—Submachine gun.

SOI—Signal Operating Instructions. The booklet that contained the call signs and radio frequencies of the units in Vietnam.

SOP—Standard Operating Procedure.

STEEL POT—Standard U.S. Army helmet. The steel pot was the outer metal cover.

TEAM UNIFORM OR COMPANY UNIFORM— UHF radio frequency on which the team or the company communicates. Frequencies were changed periodically in an attempt to confuse the enemy.

THREE—Radio call sign of operations officer.

THREE CORPS—Military area around Saigon. Vietnam was divided into four corps areas.

TRIPLE A—Antiaircraft artillery or AAA. This is anything used to shoot at airplanes and helicopters.

THE WORLD—The United States.

TOC—Tactical Operations Center.

TOT—Time Over Target. It refers to the time that the aircraft is supposed to be over the drop zone with the parachutists, or the target if the plane is a bomber.

TWO—Radio call sign of the intelligence officer.

TWO-OH-ONE (201) FILE—Military records file that listed all of a soldier's qualifications, training, experience and abilities. It was passed from unit to unit so that the new commander would have some idea about the capabilities of an incoming soldier.

UMZ—Ultramilitarized Zone. It was the name GIs gave to the DMZ (Demilitarized Zone).

UNIFORM—Refers to the UHF radio. Company Uniform would be the frequency assigned to that company.

VC—Vietcong, called Victor Charlie (phonetic alphabet) or just Charlie.

VIETCONG—Contraction of Vietnam Cong Sam (Vietnamese Communist).

VIETCONG SAN—Vietnamese Communists. A term in use since 1956.

WHITE MICE—Referred to the Vietnamese military police because they all wore white helmets.

WHITE SIDE WALLS—A style of haircut favored by the NVA in which the sides and back of the head were shaved with a thatch left on the top of the head.

WIA—Wounded In Action.

WILLIE PETE—WP, white phosphorus, called smoke rounds. Also used as antipersonnel weapons.

WSO—Weapons System Officer. The name given to the man who rode in the back seat of a Phantom because he is responsible for the weapons systems.

XO—Executive officer of a unit.

ZAP—To ding, pop caps or shoot. To kill.

ZIPPO—Flamethrower.

**A secret arms deal
with Iran ignites a powder keg,
and a most daring mission is
about to begin.**

THE BARRABAS STRIKE

JACK HILD

Nile Barrabas and his soldiers undertake a hazardous assignment when a powerful top-secret weapon disappears and shows up in Iran.

Available in March at your favorite retail outlet, or reserve your copy for February shipping by sending your name, address, zip or postal code, along with a check or money order for $4.70 (includes 75¢ for postage and handling) payable to Gold Eagle to:

SS-1

In the U.S.	In Canada
Gold Eagle Books	Gold Eagle Books
901 Fuhrmann Boulevard	P.O. Box 609
Box 1325	Fort Erie, Ontario
Buffalo, NY 14269-1325	L2A 5X3

Please specify book title with your order.

GOLD
EAGLE ®

Take
4 explosive books
plus a
mystery bonus
FREE

Mail to **Gold Eagle Reader Service**®

In the U.S.
P.O. Box 1394
Buffalo, N.Y. 14240-1394

In Canada
P.O. Box 609
Fort Erie, Ont. L2A 5X3

YEAH! Rush me 4 free Gold Eagle novels and my free mystery
bonus. Then send me 6 brand-new novels every other month as
they come off the presses. Bill me at the low price of just $14.95 —
an 11% saving off the retail price - plus 95¢ postage and handling
per shipment. There is no minimum number of books I must buy. I
can always return a shipment and cancel at any time. Even if I never
buy another book from Gold Eagle, the 4 free novels and the
mystery bonus are mine to keep forever.   166 BPM BP7F

_____

Name   (PLEASE PRINT)

_____

Address   Apt. No.

_____

City   State/Prov.   Zip/Postal Code

_____

Signature (If under 18, parent or guardian must sign)

This offer is limited to one order per household and not valid to
present subscribers. Price is subject to change.

                                                4E-SUB-1D

TAKE 'EM NOW

FOLDING SUNGLASSES FROM GOLD EAGLE

Mean up your act with these tough, street-smart shades. Practical, too, because they fold 3 times into a handy, zip-up polyurethane pouch that fits neatly into your pocket. Rugged metal frame. Scratch-resistant acrylic lenses. Best of all, they can be yours for only $6.99.
MAIL YOUR ORDER TODAY.

Send your name, address, and zip code, along with a check or money order for just $6.99 + .75¢ for postage and handling (for a total of $7.74) payable to Gold Eagle Reader Service. (New York and Iowa residents please add applicable sales tax.)

Remove from pouch...

unfold once...

Gold Eagle Reader Service
901 Fuhrmann Blvd.
P.O. Box 1396
Buffalo, N.Y. 14240-1396

unfold twice...

and they're ready to wear.

Offer not available in Canada.